Brave young monster detective Will Allen may have conquered his fears, but can he prevail in his latest battle when his monster–fighting weapons turn against him?

Instead of fending off the monsters, the whip recoiled, arising and squirming about like a snake…

And then it *was* a snake – the end of the whip sprouted a serpent head that hissed and snapped in every direction. But then it spotted me, and reared itself into a coil.

"N-nice snake," I said gently. "Good snake…Um, Polly want a cracker?"

Yes, I know that was lame. I don't know why I said that – it just somehow spilled out of my mouth. The snake hissed again, and then lunged at me, snapping its jaws inches from my face.

"Remember," I whispered to myself. "It just wants to scare me. Monsters won't do any real harm…"

It was just as I was speaking those words that the snake lunged forward again, and its fangs bit deep into my flesh. I screamed.

Now when you are standing with a monster-snake thrashing about while its fangs are sunk into your arm, all bets are off. You'll do pretty much anything to get loose, and that includes swinging your arm wildly, smacking the head of the snake with anything you can get your hands on, and cussing with words that would get you a gazillion detentions if they were ever heard in school. Finally, one wild swing of my arm sent the head of the snake flying across the room. But it clearly wasn't done with me, as it coiled itself back up and quickly slithered in my direction. It hissed, and lunged at me again…

ISBN 10 : 0978951247
ISBN 13 : 9780978951245

Library of Congress Catalog # 2012943330

Printed in the U.S.A.

First Printing - Halloween 2012

CPSC Product Tracking Information available at
http://roguebearpress.com/custom4.html

This book is rated level III in the Rogue Bear Press AcceleReader Program.
It is designed for children 8 - 15 years of age.
Learn more about our AcceleReader Program at our website,
RogueBearPress.com.

Teachers and Librarians take note :
Special sales discounts are offered to schools and libraries.
Discounts are available for purchases of as little as 5 copies.
Major purchases can be accompanied by a free author visit/assembly program.
Check our website for details about our discount programs and school visits.
Or contact us at Programs@RogueBearPress.com

JASON EDWARDS

The Chronicles of the
Volume
3
MONSTER DETECTIVE AGENCY

Rogue Bear Press
New York

To Jenna and Jessica,

And to all of you who take up the struggle
to find the best in yourselves and others

**More Monster Detective Agency adventures
from** JASON EDWARDS :

Will Allen and the Great Monster Detective

Will Allen and the Ring of Terror

Will Allen and the Hideous Shroud

Will Allen and the Terrible Truth

Will Allen and the Unconquerable Beast

Will Allen and the Dubious Shrine

Will Allen and the Lair of the Phantoms

Will Allen and the Greatest Mystery of All

Contents

Chapter One - Terms

First of all, let's get one thing straight – the name is Will. Will Allen. It's not Bill, Billy, William, or 'the Willster'. It's not 'Little Jimmy Neutron', like some kids at school call me, or 'Say Hey Willie' like my dad shouts out every time I come up to bat in little league. It is *definitely* not Doofus Dorkenstein, like some of the brainless jocks call me, and it is absolutely, positively not...

"Hilmar?" the substitute homeroom teacher called out. "Hilmar Allen?"

"Will," my best friend, Jeannine Fitsimmons, said after elbowing me in the ribs. "I think she means *you*."

"What?" I mumbled.

"She's taking the attendance. I think she just called out your name."

"No..." I gasped. "She didn't call out..."

"Hilmar Allen!" the teacher shouted over the chatter filling the classroom. "Present or absent?"

I put my hands over my mouth and gasped. My eyes widened in shock as I realized that one of my worst nightmares had just come true. For a moment, I thought about just letting the teacher mark me absent. Anything would be better than admitting the truth about...that *name*.

"My name is Will," I finally grumbled.

"What? What was that?"

"It's Will," I growled louder. "*Will* Allen. I'm present."

"But where's Hilmar?"

Now just so you know, I have a lot of respect for teachers. In fact, not counting Mrs. McCallister from Math class, some of my favorite people are teachers.

But obviously, this lady wasn't the sharpest tool in the shed, if you know what I mean. The qualifications for being a substitute teacher in my school must be pretty low.

"There is no Hilmar!" I shouted. "There's just me. Will. Will Allen."

"I'm sorry, but the attendance sheet says Hilmar."

Snickering began hammering my ears. I looked around the room and saw kids pointing at me and giggling. Even the stupid cartoon alphabet figures hung along the top of the blackboard seemed to be laughing. My eyes began to burn, either from the glare of the stark florescent light bouncing off the walls, or from the realization that ten years of carefully guarding my secret had just gone right down the tubes.

"Fine," I conceded, dropping my head into my hands. "Just mark me present."

But as I sat there pounding my temples, a strong odor, kind of like a cross between spoiled cheese and old socks, suddenly stung my nose. It quickly grew stronger, signaling that something foul was approaching.

"Hilmar?" sneered a familiar, oily voice just as I felt a hard slap on my back. "Really? *Hilmar*? Nice freakin' name, Dorkenstein."

I turned and looked up, and found a mess of stringy black hair and a large hooked nose lording high over my head. Now, I'm kind of used to looking up at people's heads, seeing as how I'm one of the shortest kids in school, but this shaggy lump made my hair stand on end. It was propped upon shoulders covered by an Ashford Middle School football team jacket with a navy front, maroon sleeves, and a bold letter 'A' on the chest, but you wouldn't think he was an athlete from the look of him – he was as sloppy as an unmade bed and his movements were awkward and twitchy. But if you saw the nasty glint in his eye, you'd never have any doubt that he was a bully.

And if you *did* have doubts about that, trust me; I know it from personal experience.

"Get lost, Jacko," I barked. "You're the last person who should make fun of someone's name." And then I turned back around.

Several kids around us gaped or howled, "OOooowww!" Jacko spluttered and blinked a few times, but then came around and got right in my face.

"*What?*" he growled. "You're mouthing off at me, Dorkenstein? *You?* You can't talk to me like that!"

He pounded his hands down on my desk and leaned toward me, but I stared right into his mousy little eyes and replied, "Obviously, genius, I *can*. I just did."

Jacko staggered as if I had hit him with a brick (Oh, if only…). He recovered himself, and grabbed my shirt and tried to pull me close, but I was braced against the desk, and didn't budge. Jacko shook his head in confusion, then his mouth started opening and closing like a fish, and his squinty eyes flickered like an old light bulb. A very *dim* light bulb.

"You - I'll…I'll bust your freakin'…" he began to say.

Jeannine leaned toward us and shouted, "Hey, let him go!" But before she could even get up…

"Is there a problem?" called out the substitute teacher.

Jacko blinked, but I kept staring right at him. He let go of my shirt and mumbled, "Um, no…no problem." But before he went back to his seat, he whispered, "Just you wait, runt," into my ear.

I turned and glared at him as he shuffled away like an old man, hunched over as if his head was too heavy to hold up. My bet is that's because it's filled with lead instead of brains. But even though he was probably too dense to hold a thought for very long, he was definitely nasty enough to hold a grudge for just about forever, so there wasn't much doubt that he would try to get back at me.

But I wasn't scared of him anymore. In fact, the only thing that frightened me was that word would get around about my true name. The thought of people calling me Hilmar the rest of my life is scarier than facing the most horrifying monster.

And I should know.

I bit my lip and groaned in frustration. For years, I had made a point of getting to every teacher before they read my name out loud and letting them know that they should call me Will. But I was so distracted that morning that I hadn't even noticed that there was a sub until it was too late. You see, my friend Jeannine had just begun telling me a wild story about how she single-handedly fought a raging battle against horrible, blood-curdling monsters. Of course, I couldn't believe it – I mean, why hadn't she called me in for backup?

You see, Jeannine and I are monster detectives. Now I know that sounds like some Xbox game or crazy fantasy to you, but it's not. Monsters are real. Real enough to bite your head off and use it as a bowling ball if you don't conquer them before they grow too strong. Jeannine and I work together as partners in our own Monster Detective Agency, but thanks to my mom and Gerald Hoffsteadler, Jeannine had to face this latest horror alone.

Wait, I'm not making sense, am I? Sorry. Jumping ahead when I tell stories is a bad habit of mine, you know, kind of like nose picking.

No, I didn't mean that *I'm* a nose picker. I was just making a point about...oh, never mind. The point is – this stuff is kind of hard for me to explain.

Let me put it another way – try picturing this: dangerous villains are running wild through the streets, looting and pillaging, causing fear and panic. Somewhere, a brave superhero quickly changes into his costume to get ready to go save the city. But just as he is about to run off to battle the evildoers, his mom waves her finger and says, "Uh, uh - You can't go…you're grounded, remember?"

Sounds crazy, right? Well, welcome to my world.

OK, to explain all this properly, I need to go back a bit. It all started the night that Jeannine and I solved the case of the Ring of Terror (Jeannine named it that – I just call it the case where Timmy Newsome squealed like a little girl). Now, fighting monsters isn't like a football game – it doesn't end when time runs out, so I was a little late getting back home from Timmy's house. Forty-five minutes past my curfew, to be exact. And my mom was sitting in the kitchen waiting for me when I walked into the house.

"Sit," she called out the moment I came through the door. The air was thick with the scent of disinfectant and bleach as I stepped into the kitchen and saw her slumped in her chair with a spray bottle and a filthy dust rag in her hands. Her dirty-blonde curls hung loosely around her face from a very tired-looking bandana.

"Wow. Everything looks so clean," I said. My mom didn't answer. Now, my mother only does night-time house cleaning when she's really tense or upset, which meant that it was a good time for the neighbors to put on their sound-dampening headphones, because I was about to get an earful. The flowery plastic slipcover on the kitchen chair squealed as I tried to sit down quietly and sink as deep as I could into the huge trench coat and bowler hat I was wearing – the monster detective uniform I'd put together from old clothes I'd found in the attic. When my mom finally looked up, she glared at me the same as the monster in Timmy's bedroom had done, except that the monster's eyes were a little softer.

"Do you know what time it is?" she hissed.

I just nodded, and looked around. "Where's Dad?"

"Never you mind, mister!" my mom shouted, slamming her hands to the table, making an imprint in the freshly waxed surface. "Do you have any idea how worried I've been?"

"You were worried? Why? You don't believe that the

monsters I fight are real, so what could you have been worried about?"

"Oh, don't throw that rubbish of yours at me!" she shrieked, popping up from the table and rising above me. "You could have been anywhere! You could have been lying in a gutter for all I knew!"

I shrank back from her blistering screams. Let me tell you - if I ever want my head bitten off, there is never a need for me to wait around for monsters to do it.

"I...I told you I was going to Timmy Newsome's house. You could have just called them..."

Thankfully, that bit of logic acted like a splash of cold water in my mom's face. She instantly quieted, except for the sound of her teeth grinding. Her eyes closed, and she inhaled a long, loud breath. As the air whistled into her lungs, she waved her arms in a circle and brought her hands together as though she was praying (which is exactly what *I* felt like doing), then backed away and sat back down in her seat at the table.

"You're grounded," she said flatly as her eyes slowly reopened.

"But…but don't you even want to know why I'm late?" I asked.

"Does it have anything to do with that ridiculous monster hunting thing you say you're doing?"

"Actually, yes," I said proudly. "Jeannine and me, we just solved our first case together! See, Timmy Newsome was being haunted by this terrible harpy that was…"

"Then *no*, I don't want to know why you're late," she said. "Grounded. Two days. School. Home. Your room. That's it. And no phone, video games, or TV."

"Two days?" I gasped. "But…but doesn't it count for something that I saved someone from horrifying monsters? That I faced terrible danger and came home safe and sound?"

My mother studied me thoughtfully.

"Yes, that does count for something," she muttered, tapping her index finger to a spot on her chin that was already worn and red as she stared into space. She tapped some more, and then looked back down at me.

"Make it *three* days," she said. "Now go get yourself cleaned up! You look like you've been playing in a land fill. And don't you dare throw those filthy clothes on the floor. I just mopped it." And she then stormed off, muttering under her breath, "They never taught us about things like this in child psychology class…"

I just sat there, feeling as frustrated as the day I got punished for throwing up all over my mom's new carpet (Hey, *she* was the one who insisted that I eat those asparagus dumplings she made). But I guess I couldn't really expect any better: after all, I *was* out past my curfew. And seeing as how grown-ups can't even *see* kids' monsters, I honestly couldn't expect my mom to believe that the reason I got home late was because I was too busy helping Timmy Newsome fend off a gruesome harpy while dodging spears of flame that came from his father's wedding ring.

Even though it was the truth. But then as any kid knows, grownups have no use for a truth they don't want to hear.

"This is just so unfair," I muttered as I stood and strode into the living room on the way to the stairs.

"What was that?" a voice called out from deep within the cushions of the easy chair by the far wall. My eyes followed the voice across the room, over the pristine leather couch that is so beautiful that no one is allowed to sit on it, and past the exotic coffee table shaped like a series of interlocking snakes. Behind the table, above a stack of neatly laid out art books that are the only items in the whole house with dust on them, sat a rickety old lounger that clashed with all of the other furniture in the room. Spread open wide in front of the chair was an upright newspaper that blocked from view all but the hands of the person who sat holding it.

"I said it's not fair, Dad!" I barked at the back of the sports section. The newspaper didn't flinch, but the chair's vinyl cushions groaned as my father leaned forward to speak.

"Well, Will," my dad's voice began, "It's about time you learned that…"

"Life's not fair, so I better get used to it," I recited. "I know."

The newspaper ruffled, and then dropped several inches, revealing thinning grey hair, a broad, ruddy forehead, and finally, my dad's puzzled eyes.

"How did you know I was going to say that?" he asked. I just rolled my eyes.

"The same way I knew where to find your missing golf club or what that rattling sound was in the back of the car. I'm a detective, Dad!"

My father chuckled, "No, really…" I frowned at him.

"All right, Dad," I replied. "The real reason I knew you'd say that is because it's what you *always* say. It's the same thing you told me after I got picked on by that bully."

My father's eyes squinted for a second, but then he lifted the paper back up.

"Well, that's because it's true," he said, and then the cushions made a splooshy sound as he settled back into them. He didn't speak again, and I didn't feel like talking to the back of the newspaper, so I continued to the stairs and up to my room.

Chapter Two - Turnabout

When I got to my room, I stumbled in, tossed my ratty bowler hat over to my desk, and plopped down, face first, onto my bed without so much as taking off my shoes and coat.

Hey, you'd be tired too if you'd just been struggling with horrifying, insufferable creatures.

And that's after fighting monsters all night.

But even though I was exhausted, I couldn't help tossing and turning in my bed.

"Grounded!" I grumbled as I sat up, arms crossed. Around me the walls of my room, which are normally sickeningly cheery-looking, brooded darkly in the moonlight. "Grounded for doing good! Punished for being a hero! It's so unfair!"

Still, the more I sat there moping, the more I knew that there was nothing I could do to change my parents' minds, and no point in whining about it either. I squirmed weakly a bit, but then resolved, as I lay back down and my eyes began to flutter closed, that I would simply take my punishment quietly.

When I come home tomorrow, I'll just go right to my room, I thought as my mind grew fuzzy. *At least then I'll be able to catch up on my schoolwork.* And I would have done just that, but for the card.

That would be my special, Monster Detective Agency business card. It's the card that magically appears to kids who have a monster, telling them to come to me, Will Allen, monster detective third class, to get help. Only somehow the card got all mixed up, because the next time it appeared, it sent Gerald Hoffsteadler to...

Hold on. I'm jumping ahead again. Just wait – we'll get to that part in a minute.

So anyway, the next morning started out pretty much like most every other day: with the shrill whine of my alarm clock making me stuff my head under the pillow. My hand banged its way blindly across the end table until it either hit the snooze button or smashed the buzzer, I'm not sure which. My eyes were still half shut as I rolled out of bed and threw off my Chicago Cubs bedspread, which had somehow wrapped itself around me as I slept, then staggered over to the window and opened the shades to let the sun wake up the bright blue walls of my room. I made my bed (sort of), and then tottered down the hall to the bathroom to wash up. I splashed my face, but when I looked up from the sink I gasped in horror at my reflection.

"Oh no!" I whispered to myself as the mirror revealed that I was still wearing my slimy monster detective clothes from the night before. "If mom finds out she'll... "

"Will, are you awake?" My mother's voice rang out at that very moment.

"No!" I shouted back, but then slapped my mouth closed.

Yes, I know that's like locking the barn door after the horse has escaped, but I couldn't help myself. I peeked out the door to make sure no one was in the hallway, then quickly scooted back to my room. With the fog washed from my eyes, the morning light spreading through my room showed that monster slime, which had splattered on my jacket during the previous night's adventure, had dripped all over my bed and floor. I grabbed a dirty towel from my hamper and wiped up the trail of goo, then cleaned off my hair, face, and hands too, just in case. After all, you don't think I would go to school looking like a slob, do you?

Wait. Don't answer that.

Next, I changed my clothes, putting on my chinos and a rugby shirt, and then combed my hair and brushed my teeth as usual. But after that there was still one more chore to perform. I cautiously drew on over to a large glass fishbowl on my shelf which was half-filled with dirt, grass, and leaves. It shook a little as I approached, and as I drew closer, something under the leaves rustled. I leaned in for a better look, when suddenly a set of vicious fangs sprang from the underbrush and snapped hard at my face. The glistening teeth smacked up against the inside of the bowl as it tried to chomp at me; teeth set in jaws that were not framed in a face, but rather by a tiny basin and lid attached to a ceramic tank. Crowning the tank, two round eyes topped by bushy brows scowled at me. As the fanged bowl gnashed and bit at the glass, two more little creatures came out from under the leaves: an inch long shark that flopped its way across the terrain on its belly, and a miniature tree with tiny flower buds on its branches that crawled along on gnarled roots. These were the toilet, tree, and shark monsters that I shrank to thimble-size in my first adventure, and even though they used to be huge, scary monsters, they seemed almost cute now, kind of like little baby chicks.

Well, actually more like little baby Tyrannosaurs, but still cute.

"Good morning, boys!" I called out cheerfully. I tapped the glass, and I swear the tiny shark-monster purred a little. Now, there's no owner's manual for pet monsters, so I threw in some small, unwrapped Halloween candies in case they got hungry, and then dropped an old toy into the bowl for them to play with – some stupid Polly Pocket doll that got put in my Happy-Meal by mistake. Then I headed downstairs to breakfast.

It was quiet when I walked into the kitchen. My dad was in his usual spot, sitting in his chair, hiding behind the morning paper, and my mother was emptying dishes from the dishwasher. No one said anything, but I guess my mom must have still been mad at me, because she handed me something thick, creamy, and green to drink.

"Is this part of my punishment?" I asked as I stared uneasily at the small, dark bits swirling inside the glass.

"No, of course not," my mother said. "For your information, that is a healthy breakfast smoothie. It's delicious and nutritious. So drink up."

I sniffed it to test it out, but that only gave me a sudden urge to vomit, so I held my nose and took a sip. Well, my mom may have called it a healthy breakfast smoothie, but a better name for it would have been toxic sludge. And even though she said it wasn't part of my punishment, it might just as well have been. Of course, my mom wouldn't let me leave the house until I finished the drink, so I finally managed to 'accidentally' spill much of it down the drain, which probably put me on our plumber's *most wanted* list. Still, I ended up running late, and having to sprint down the block to catch the school bus just before it drove off without me. Again.

"Come on - move it!" growled the driver as I dashed through the door. Now, our school bus driver is a no-nonsense kind of woman who looks like she was meant to be in the marines, what with her navy uniform, husky build, and flat, grim-looking face.

"Hurry up!" she barked. "You're making me late, as usual."

"Good," I replied breathlessly as I hopped up the steps. "I don't want to ruin my perfect record."

"Just find yourself a seat!" she hissed, and then, as I started down the aisle I heard her mutter, "Smart alecky kids! They don't pay me enough for this…"

I took a moment to catch my breath, then continued down the aisle. Jeannine was already there in her usual seat, seven rows back next to the emergency escape. But even if I didn't know where to look for her, I would have spotted her in an instant, seeing as how she had added bright, rainbow-colored streaks to her hair again. She smiled and waved me over as though I wasn't already going to sit right next to her, just as I have ever since third grade.

"So, how are we feeling today, Mister Monster Detective?" she whispered cheerfully as I parked myself in the seat beside her. I had to twist a bit as I sat so as not to land on some dangling, multi-colored scarves she had tied around the waistband of her sea-green jeans like a belt. That, combined with the tie-dyed blouse and plastic beaded necklaces she wore made her outfit look a little like a broken neon sign.

"Fine, Miss Monster Detective," I replied softly, looking around as I did to make sure no one was listening.

"That's *Ms.* Monster Detective, thank you very much!"

"Right. *Ms.* Monster Detective. Got it."

For some reason, Jeannine turned and studied me carefully.

"You know, for a person who just defeated horrible monsters and solved your first case, you don't look too cheerful. What's the matter?"

"Ah, I got grounded by my mom for getting home late last night."

"Well, we expected that, didn't we?"

"Yeah. But it still stinks. Three days! That's way too harsh for just being a few minutes late. My mom was way out of line, and my dad was no help at all. And then to top it off, that bus driver is a real crank."

"I know," she answered sympathetically. "And the way she dresses! Navy pants and black shoes with white socks? What was she thinking? With her build and complexion, she'd look much better in silk and tartan."

I glared at her.

"What?"

"Nothing," I said. "I just forget sometimes about your...eh, your artistic taste in clothes."

Jeannine nodded.

"I get that from my grandmother," she said. "She was quite the Bohemian in her time."

"Quite the what?"

Jeannine smiled.

"Oh, I'm sorry," she said slyly. "I forgot that you don't have quite as advanced a vocabulary as I do."

"*What?*"

"Not that you aren't way ahead of the average 6th grader, mind you," she soothed. "But still, you're not quite at my..."

"Um, could we just get back to the whole '*what in the world is a Bohemian*' thing?" I interrupted.

"Oh, of course. A Bohemian is someone who is free-spirited or lives an unusual lifestyle. You know, like artists, writers, musicians, and actors."

"Thank you very much, Miss Dictionary."

"That's *Ms.* Dictionary."

"Right. *Ms.* Dictionary."

I took a moment then and scanned the bus up and down.

"So, where's Timmy Newsome?" I asked. "He's not on the bus today. You think he's too tired from...our little adventure?"

"Oh no, he's getting a ride from his dad today. It seems they have a lot to talk about."

I smiled.

"Well, it's nice to know we... hold on, how did you know that?"

Jeannine's eyes darted for a second, and she began brushing her legs off like she had spilled something.

"Oh, well...he called me last night, you know, to thank me for saving him and all, and we got to talking."

"Really? He didn't call to say 'thank you' to *me*."

"Well, you know, it was pretty late when we were done talking. He probably thought you were asleep."

"Hmmm," I hummed thoughtfully. I probably *was* asleep, but I was pretty sure that wasn't the reason that Jeannine got a call and I didn't.

Well anyway, after that we talked about this and that...blah, blah, blah - all the usual stuff, until the bus arrived at school. Actually, Jeannine did most of the talking. In fact, she kept chattering the whole time from the bus to our lockers to homeroom. I spent most of that time rushing through the homework I was supposed to have done the night before, but I kept nodding my head now and then as she spoke, so Jeannine barely noticed. Once the bell rang and class began though, we settled into our usual routine.

But then, without warning, something happened that turned my day upside down.

It all began during lunch. Normally when the lunch bell sounds I go to my locker, exchange my books for my lunch box, and grumble to myself about whatever horrible excuse for food my mother packed me. After that, it's on to the lunch room, where I plop myself down at the table nearest the recycling bins in the second seat from the end: the same spot Jeannine and I have been sitting in since September. It's a great spot, except for the broken plastic seat, but if you sit down carefully, you don't get jabbed by the shards. Not that it matters, because this day I didn't even make it to the cafeteria, and for once it didn't have anything to do with the horrible smell coming from my lunch box. You see, I had barely shut my locker and started down the hall when my eyes caught sight of Jeannine. She was standing against the wall near the exit to the cafeteria, which was odd because Jeannine doesn't buy any cafeteria food: she always gets stuck with some disgusting lunch that her mother prepared for her, just like me.

Now that I think about it, it's pretty funny that Jeannine and I fight monsters, but both of our mothers were clearly trained to cook by one.

Anyway, as I got closer I could see that Jeannine wasn't alone. She was talking intently to a short, scrawny, freckle-faced boy with frizzy hair wearing mismatched clothes and oversized glasses. He looked like a real dork, what with his shirt half untucked and a pocket protector hanging from his belt.

And no matter what anybody tells you, that is not what *I* look like – for one thing, I don't have a pocket protector, freckles, or glasses.

OK, you're right. That's *three* things.

Anyway, I couldn't hear anything over the noise of the hallway, but I could see that he was waving his hands wildly as he talked, and for a second I thought I might have to run over to protect Jeannine, but then I saw her look him squarely in the eye and say something with a stern expression on her face, and he backed away, fidgeting nervously. Jeannine leaned in and spoke again, then put her hand on his shoulder, and he finally seemed to calm down. She spoke one more time, they both nodded, and then Jeannine walked off. The boy's eyes followed her at first, but then he turned and walked off in the other direction, quickly disappearing into the mass of kids mulling about all through the corridor.

"Hey!" I said casually as I walked up to her. "Where's your lunch?"

Jeannine didn't answer.

"Was that guy bothering you? Because if he was, I'll…"

But I stopped in mid-sentence, because Jeannine had lifted her hand and was extending it to me. In her fingers was a small piece of paper, the size of an ordinary business card, but this one hummed with hidden energy.

"Is - is that…?"

Jeannine nodded her head.

"He had one of our business cards? That boy has a…"

Jeannine quickly smacked me in the mouth. I'm sure she only meant to put her hand over my lips to muffle me, but her aim isn't very good when she doesn't have her glasses on, so it ended up more like an uppercut to the jaw.

"Mmmerfff! Hey! What are you…"

"Shhh," she whispered. "We're supposed to be keeping all this a secret, remember?"

"Oh, right," I nodded, then looked around. "Come on. This way."

We stepped around the corner and into an alcove by the broken water fountain.

"So, show me!" I whispered excitedly.

But Jeannine held the card back.

"Um…You may not like what you see," she said.

"What? What are you talking about?" I growled. Jeannine hesitated, but then handed me the card. It read:

"Hey!" I cried. "What gives? My name's not on here!"

Jeannine looked down, but when she saw me staring at her, she just shrugged.

"Maybe it's because you gave me the MonsterScope last

night," she offered. "Maybe it's only the name of the person who has the scope that appears on the card."

"*Both* of our names were on the card last night," I reminded her. "Both of our names were there even when you didn't think that you were cut out to be a detective. And that was before I gave you the MonsterScope."

Jeannine nodded, and then started scratching her head, which to me is even worse than nose-picking.

"Maybe the card knows you're grounded," she suggested.

"That's ridiculous," I grumbled. "The card *knows* things?"

"Well, it knew that I was going to be a detective even before I did, didn't it?" Jeannine said, her tone suddenly huffy. "And if it *knows* when someone needs help, then why couldn't it know when someone *can* help?"

I just stared at her.

"OK, maybe," I finally conceded. "So then tell me the rest. Who was that? And what did he tell you about his…"

I stopped and looked around to make sure no one was listening.

"…His you-know-what?"

Jeannine looked surprised.

"You don't know Gerald? Gerald Hoffsteadler?"

I shook my head. "Should I?"

"Well, it's just that he's…I mean the two of you are so similar that I figured you must know each other."

My eyes narrowed.

"Similar? In what way?"

Jeannine fidgeted a bit before answering, "Well, he's short, skinny, has no sense of style…"

"*Excuse* me?" I fumed, but Jeannine just carried on.

"…he's shy, he likes math class even more than recess…"

"I like *science*…"

"…he gets picked on by bigger, meaner kids, and he has a monster in his closet. Does any of this sound familiar?"

"He's not like me!" I insisted.

"Oh, come on Will!" Jeannine scoffed. "He's more like you than *you* are! Except that he doesn't have a Great Monster Detective like Bigelow Hawkins to help him face his monsters. He has us."

I didn't answer. I just stood there glaring at her.

"So, are you going to just stand there fuming?" Jeannine blurted.

"I am not fuming!" I lied, even though my cheeks were turning flame red. That's what happens when I get angry, so believe me, when I'm mad everybody knows it.

"Oh, *please*," Jeannine retorted. Your cheeks are so fired up that you could fry an egg on your face. Of course, that would still be an improvement over what I've got in my lunchbox."

I tried to stay mad, but she got me laughing, as always. Jeannine joined in, and when the last spurts of giggles finally died out, I was calm again.

"Yeah, all right," I said. "So, when are we going to go check this monster out?"

"*We* aren't checking it out," Jeannine said flatly. "*I'm* checking it out. You're grounded, remember?"

"What?" I sputtered. "Oh…oh, right. But you can wait for me, right? You're not going to go *tonight*?"

"Well actually, I told Gerald that I would do it tomorrow night. I've got plans this afternoon in the city, and I won't get back until late."

"Plans? How come you didn't tell me about them?"

"Oh, it's nothing. It's just another one of those auditions my mother found out about in Variety magazine. You know how she is: She keeps saying that, with my talent, one day I'll land a big role and become a rich and famous actress."

I snickered.

"I'm sorry, did I say something funny?" Jeannine's voice was mellow but her eyes hollered like a banshee.

"It's not you," I soothed. "It's your mom. Don't you think it's funny that she's so much more into that whole thing than you are?"

"Oh, don't get me started..."

"I won't! I won't! Anyway, I'm sure you'll do great. You always do. All of your shows are terrific."

Actually, that was only partly true. Jeannine is my friend, and she's actually a pretty good actress, but sitting through one of those school plays is torture.

"Well, I hope so," she grumbled. "I'd hate to think I'm leaving Gerald at the mercy of some monster just to sit in a crowded room waiting for the chance to spend two seconds with some casting director."

"Well now that you mention it, if you can put off investigating this case for one day because of this audition, why not put it off two more days so that I can come with you?"

"And let Gerald be terrorized by his monster three more days? You didn't see his face – he needs help as soon as possible! But I *have to* go to this audition. My mom won't let me miss it."

"Yeah, but..."

"And anyway, the card had *my* name on it, Will. Just mine. It doesn't seem like it's meant for you to go."

"Not meant for me to go?!" I growled. "You must be kidding me! *Your* name wasn't on the card yesterday afternoon, but that didn't stop you from coming to fight Timmy's monster!"

"That was different. You needed my help."

"Don't you think you need *my* help?! You're facing monsters you know!"

"Oh, Will, stop worrying!" Jeannine insisted. "It's not like I'm going to be in any *real* danger."

"No real danger?" I sputtered. "Are you nuts? You don't call facing horrible monsters and maybe getting eaten alive *danger?*"

"Oh, re*lax*," she said. "What's the big deal? The monsters only want to scare us."

"Oh really? What makes you so sure that's all they want to do?"

"Well, it just makes sense, doesn't it? That's all the monsters at Timmy's house really did, even though they could have probably done much worse to us if they wanted."

"You think they didn't *try* to do worse...?" I argued, but Jeannine was on a roll again, and at this point she seemed to barely even notice that I was there.

"...And so I asked myself why that was," she continued as though I hadn't even spoken. "And I realized that if the monsters feed off of our fears like you told me they do, they need to keep us alive. They're like, you know – parasites. They couldn't very well feed off of our fears if we've been eaten, could they? So they make themselves look scary, and growl and snap at us, but don't do any real harm."

Jeannine finally stopped to catch a breath, and I wanted to use that moment to point out the flaws in her reasoning, but I had to admit that what she said made sense. After all, if me, Jeannine, and Timmy had all survived facing man-eating monsters without so much as a scratch, then maybe the monsters weren't as dangerous as they seemed, or they weren't trying too hard. And although I didn't like the idea of her going to face monsters alone, she was right about another thing too. My monster detective mentor, Detective Bigelow Hawkins, the Great Monster Detective, told me that monsters don't actually eat flesh: they feed off of our fears, so it makes sense that they would want to frighten us, not eat us.

"I guess you're right," I conceded.

"Of course I am," she said, beaming with satisfaction.

"But I still don't like it," I said sharply. Jeannine broke into an even bigger smile.

"*I* do," she said.

Chapter Three - Disturbances

Needless to say, I was not in a good mood the rest of the day. Even finding out that my mother had ordered in pizza because she was too busy to cook did nothing to improve my spirits.

"Are you ill?" my mom asked when I pushed my plate away. "I mean this is pepperoni – your favorite!"

"Not hungry…" I muttered.

"Are you sure?" she said as she slowly waved a slice under my nose.

"Um, well…maybe just a bite."

Hey, when the food isn't poisonous, you've got to fill up no matter what mood you're in. Three slices later, my stomach was full, but I still felt glum. I trudged up to my room, so dazed by the questions burning in my mind that I missed the first step of the stairs and stumbled back, tripped over the easy chair, fell through the open newspaper my dad was holding, and landed on his lap. Finding himself abruptly face to face with me made my dad wince uncomfortably.

Or, to be fair, it might have been because my knee had crashed sharply into his…well, you know.

"Uhhhhmmmm," he squeaked. "Is there something on your mind?"

As you can guess, that conversation did not go well.

A lecture or two later, I finally made it back to my room.

My dad had taken a lot of bad guesses about what was bothering me, so he went on and on talking about things like propriety (whatever that is), courage (which I'm way past needing help with) and responsibility (like I care). But he was right about one thing – there *was* something on my mind.

But he was not the one I needed answers from.

"Bigelow?" I called out. "Bigelow Hawkins? Can you hear me?"

All day I had wanted to talk to my mentor, Bigelow Hawkins, the Great Monster Detective, to thank him for the advice that guided me through the maze of mysteries and dangers I faced at Timmy's house, and to let him know how the case turned out. But now there was much more on my mind than that: I wanted...no, *needed* to ask him whether it would be safe for Jeannine to be facing monsters without my help. I had to know that everything would be OK.

"Bigelow? Are you out there?"

But there was no answer. For a moment, I bit my lip, but then I suddenly snapped my fingers. I ran over to my dresser, dug down into the bottom of the last drawer, and pulled out a t-shirt that was completely covered with blotchy, purplish stains. It was the shirt that I drenched in fruit punch so that I could use it to summon Bigelow the first time I called on him. There was no way I was going to put that stained shirt in the laundry for my mother to find, so it's been hidden deep in my dresser ever since. I shook it out, then tied it to my baseball bat and hung it out my window.

"OK, Bigelow," I bellowed. "You can come out now."

But nothing happened.

"Um, Bigelow Hawkins: appear!"

Still nothing.

"Ah, let me see...Oh, Great Monster Detective, I summon you!"

This time, there was a response. But not the one I was looking for.

"What's going on up there?" my mother shouted from down in the kitchen.

"Ah, nothing Mom," I called back. "I'm not doing anything."

"Well do nothing more quietly!" she growled.

"Right. Quietly," I muttered. Then I sat back down on my bed. That was when I noticed that my Teddy Bear was missing. Well actually, it's Bigelow's Teddy Bear now, seeing as how that was his payment for helping me conquer my first monsters. Still, the bear had been sitting on my bed next to my pillow ever since our adventure together. Now, in its place was a note that read:

Gone fishing. Back in a few days.

At first, I just stared at the note.

"Oh, terrific," I finally grumbled. "Could this day get any worse?"

"Will," my mother called out. "Get in the bath! I won't have you going another day looking like you just rolled out of a dumpster!"

I decided to go to bed early that night.

The next day was even worse. I don't want to bore you with stuff that's not important, so let's just say that there was more getting yelled at (by my dad about that fruit punch-stained shirt – I'd forgotten that I'd left it hanging in my window), more arguing (with Jeannine about waiting for me to come along to face Gerald's monster), more terrible food (my mom must have tried another recipe from the *How To Prepare Sawdust Cook Book*), and to top it off, at school I found that a big glob of ketchup had somehow been squirted into my locker. By the end of the day, I was actually relieved to go to my room and serve another evening of my punishment. I didn't want to think about the fact that Jeannine was on her way to face Gerald's monster without me. I didn't want to think about anything at all, but I had no

TV to distract me, so I set about doing the most mindless activity possible – my homework.

I was staring blankly at the English assignment that I had loaded onto my computer when my father walked in. He tried to be all quiet-like, tip-toeing up the steps and opening the door quickly so that he could catch me if I was watching TV or doing something else I wasn't allowed, but he wasn't very good at being stealthy. An elephant would stand a better chance of sneaking up on someone. And its breath would probably smell better too. I had already closed the IM message I had sent Jeannine (asking her to wait for me but insisting she tell me about everything that happened if she didn't) when he came through the door.

"It's awfully quiet up here," he said casually as he looked around the room.

"Uh huh." I mumbled. Apparently, that was not a good enough answer.

"What are you up to?" he demanded.

"Um, just doing homework," I said. My dad glanced at my desk and then glared at me suspiciously.

"On the computer?" he asked skeptically.

"That's how we do things now, Dad," I replied. "We don't do our work on stone tablets anymore."

My dad's eyes narrowed, but after several moments of painful silence, they eased.

"Fine," he said, turning back to the door, "Just remember though: no fooling around."

"Right," I said to the back of his head as he marched out the door. "No fooling around."

Twenty minutes later, I was plodding through a game on Club Penguin, marking time while waiting for Jeannine to answer my message. I knew she would be all right, after all, Bigelow had told me that the card only appears when someone is ready for what they're going to face. I was sure everything would go fine. Really.

After a while, I turned off the game, seeing as how I wasn't really paying attention to it anyway, and just stared at the computer, willing it to reply. Eventually though, my eyes grew tired of being locked on the blank message screen, and finally began to flutter.

The next thing I knew, I was dreaming.

I knew positively that it was a dream because I was *flying*. Now, lots of really weird things have been happening to me lately, but sadly, gaining the power of flight isn't one of them. Actually, now that I think about it, I wouldn't exactly call what I was doing *flying* – it was more like drifting. I couldn't soar or zoom around, but I could sort of swim along as I drifted through the air currents.

And yes, the dog-paddle *does* count as swimming.

It's hard to describe where I found myself. There was a multicolored haze in every direction, like being inside a giant tie-dyed cloud, but in the distance bits of the fog clotted to form a fuzzy background of doors and hallways. The thick mist was filled with a buzzing sound, like a thousand voices all whispering at once.

"Beware," the voices cried out, "The shadows rise." The sounds echoed around me like I was inside the Grand Canyon. Or my family's refrigerator.

"Who are you all?" I called out to the sea of voices. "What do you want?"

At that very moment, laughter sprung from somewhere deep in the darkness, cutting through the din. But it wasn't a happy, cheerful sound: it was an evil laugh, one that made my hair stand on end. Then, at once, Jeannine was there. She rose out of the fog...no, *formed* out of the fog, and her arms waved frantically, reaching out in my direction.

"Will!" she cried out in an hollow voice. "Will, help meeeee!"

Jeannine grasped at me desperately, but when I reached for her hand, it evaporated, and she disappeared back into the fog.

"Jeannine!" I cried out, swinging my head wildly back and forth to look in every direction. "Jeannine, where are you?"

I didn't hear her, but the buzz of voices surrounding me in the fog grew louder. Suddenly, a single voice rose above rest.

"Will," the voice called out softly. It was barely more than a whisper, yet in spite of all the noise it stood out as clear as day. But it wasn't Jeannine's voice, or any other one I recognized.

"Will, we are here," the voice cooed.

"Who…who are you?" I called out.

"It is your time, Will. Redeem us."

"What?" I cried, swinging my head around to try and find the speaker. "What are you talking about?"

But I still saw no one, and the voice did not answer.

Then in a blinding flash, there was light. Bright white light, so strong that it burned away the fog, the darkness, *everything*. The voices all faded away as the brightness swallowed me up completely, until nothing else existed.

I woke up with sunlight crashing down on my face. I guess I'd forgotten to close the shades before I fell asleep, so the rising sun's rays came in through my window and landed directly upon my face, waking me. I blinked furiously, and turned my head away. My hand shook as I slowly reached for my clock.

"6:30?" I mumbled groggily, dropping my head back onto the pillow without even wondering how or when I had stumbled into bed. "What am I doing up at 6:30?"

But my mind began racing, full of thoughts about my dream, and Jeannine's adventure, so I couldn't go back to sleep. Instead, I washed up, got changed (I was still wearing yesterday's clothes again – luckily, my parents don't check in on me during the night anymore), and started down the stairs. I was two steps down when I felt a burning sensation against my leg. I stopped and reached my hand into my pocket, and pulled out a small rectangle of paper. It throbbed with energy, just like my magic business card, but there was nothing written on the face of it. On the flip side, there were two words.

We Await

"What? What does that mean?" I puzzled. But once I read the words, the card turned cold. I put it back in my pocket and continued down to the living room, where my mother, already awake, sat relaxing on the loveseat in her favorite paisley robe, sipping tea.

"My, you're up early," she noted. I just nodded and walked over to the phone, and my mother's eyes followed.

"You know, I think that this punishment may have been just the thing you needed to straighten out your...wait, what do you think you're doing?"

"Calling Jeannine," I replied. My mom shook her head.

"No you are not," she said. "No phone privileges. That was part of your punishment, remember? Besides, we do not call people this early unless it's an emergency."

"But this *is* an emergency! I need to talk to her!"

"Is someone dying?"

I didn't dare answer. Actually, I didn't *know* the answer,

but my mom decided on one for me.

"Then no calling. You'll see her on the bus, anyway. Whatever it is can wait a little longer."

I frowned, but there wasn't much else I could do without getting into a big argument. Which I would only lose anyway. Instead, I went back up to my computer and checked my messages.

Nothing. And Jeannine was still off-line. I pulled out the card from my pocket again and looked it over, thinking I might make sense of its strange message, but…

"What the…" I sputtered. "It's *blank!*"

My head waved around in frustration, until something on my shelf suddenly caught my eye. I walked over to the big glass bowl, and saw my three little monsters sitting together, happily chewing. A quick check of the bowl revealed that none of the candy I had left them had been touched.

But the happy meal toy was missing.

I looked closely at the tiny saber-toothed toilet, and saw a miniature plastic arm protruding from his mouth. The crunching sound it made as he chewed tied my stomach into knots.

"Jeannine," I whispered.

Needless to say, I was in a big rush to get to the bus that morning. All morning I kept muttering "no real danger" and "the card only comes when they're ready" to myself as I made my bed, got ready for school, and went down to breakfast.

"Well, isn't this a surprise," the voice behind the newspaper perched open at the table remarked.

"No real danger," I mumbled to myself.

I was in such a hurry that I actually stuffed down the breakfast my mother prepared without so much as gagging (whatever it was, at least it wasn't still moving), and raced out the door. I got to the bus stop before anyone else, and stepped onto the bus first when it arrived. The driver did a double take.

"Who are you, and what did you do with the kid who's always making me late?"

"I'm a pod person," I replied. "We replace intelligent humans with mindless drones. But don't worry, *you* should be safe."

She glared at me, but then said, "All right, move along! You're holding up the line, and I've got a schedule to keep!"

I smiled and stepped into the aisle, but just as I passed the first seat I froze.

"Well? Move along!"

But I barely heard the driver. I had turned and looked down the aisle to see Jeannine, but she wasn't there. I checked her usual seat, but it was empty.

"Move it!" the driver shouted.

"Come on!" one of the kids waiting behind me yelled, breaking me out of my stupor. I walked back to Jeannine's seat and looked around, but there was no sign of her anywhere. In front of me were two girls in cheerleader outfits, one with unnaturally golden hair teased into fine curls and tied up with a pink ribbon on top, and the other with more natural-looking brown waves that hung down to her shoulders. The blonde girl must have been awfully eager to show off her dark tan because she wore no jacket even though it was 50 degrees outside, while her friend, who appeared very thin and pale in comparison, was smothered in a sweater with a heavy coat on top. The two took no notice of me standing in front of them as they exchanged excited whispers and squeals.

"Um, excuse me, but have either of you seen Jeannine?" I asked them.

The tan girl looked up at me and grimaced like she had suddenly gulped a mouthful of Castor Oil.

"Who?" she replied in a nasally whine, like the way my mom sounds when she has a bad cold.

"The girl who usually sits here!" I growled. "The girl who's been sitting one seat in front of you on this bus since September!"

"The freakazoid?" she replied dismissively. "Eeeewww! Why would I care?" But then she got a mischievous look in her eyes. "Wait," she added, turning to her friend, "Jaime, *you* used to be friends with her, didn't you?"

The brown-haired girl squirmed and pulled her jacket tighter around her shoulders, but then shook her head.

"Not really," she sneered. "I knew her, but she's a TWiFF."

"A what?"

"A TWiFF – Too Weird For Friending."

The blonde girl gave a nasty chuckle.

"You got that right!" she snickered. "There's something seriously wrong with that girl! And she dresses like such a skank!"

"You – Don't you talk about her like that!" I shouted. "You take that back!"

Right then, the boy sitting right behind her, who was perched forward with his arms hanging over the back of her seat, immediately stood. As he rose, he seemed to inflate like a balloon until he was about the size and shape of an upright rhinoceros. A rhino with buzz-cut blond hair, a huge square face, and wearing the same blue and maroon team jacket that Jacko McNulty and Timmy Newsome wore.

"Ay! You yelling at my girl?" he huffed menacingly.

"Ooohh, look Jaime!" the girl with the bow said gleefully. "Your boyfriend is going to kick little Jimmy Neutron's butt!"

"Shut up, Tiffany!" Jaime hissed. "He is not..." she turned and faced the boy. "I am *not* your girl!"

But he ignored her.

"I'm talkin' to you, runt!" he growled.

Well I looked from him, to her, to the rest of the kids looking on in excitement, and I kind of lost it a bit.

"I don't care!" I shouted. "My friend is missing! And you...you don't care at all! I am just so sick of all of you! You think because you're big or strong or pretty or rich or whatever, that everyone else is just..."

"Hey, what's going on back there?" the driver hollered.

"Little Jimmy Neutron here is wigging out!" Tiffany with the pink bow called out. The bus driver turned around to face us, and when she saw me she threw her hands up.

"I knew it! I knew you'd find some way to ruin my day."

"But - but I..."

"BUTTON IT!" the driver shouted. "Find yourself a seat before I radio the dispatcher to send someone to take you off this bus to a police precinct!"

"Or a mental ward," Tiffany snickered. Quiet giggles rebounded around the bus.

"WELL?"

"Fine," I grumbled, and sat down alone in Jeannine's usual seat next to the emergency exit.

That bus ride was the longest I can ever remember.

When we arrived at school, I got off the bus in a daze, bumping and bouncing my way through the crowd of kids emptying out onto the sidewalk like a beach ball. The driver saw my vacant expression and muttered, "Brain damage. It must be." I frowned, but just then a hard push from behind made me tumble down the steps of the bus. My books sprayed all over the sidewalk, but I caught myself before I hit the ground, then looked back up to see that rhino-sized boy standing on the top step of the bus, grinning nastily. I just collected my books, then turned and walked to the school entranceway, gritting my teeth. As I entered the foyer, I immediately began scanning the crowd for Jeannine, but the halls were thick with swarms of kids, cutting off my view. Being one of the shortest kids in the school, there was no way for me to peer over or around anyone, so instead I surged through the shifting mass toward Jeannine's locker, which is just a few feet from my own. She was nowhere in sight. I took a quick look inside our homeroom, but she wasn't in there either. I was really getting nervous, and began wandering the hallways looking for any sign of her.

She went to help Gerald, I thought. *If I find Gerald, he'll know what happened – he might even know where she is.*

But I didn't know where to find Gerald – and I hadn't spotted him in any of the hallways.

You two are so alike, Jeannine had said. *He likes math class more than gym...*

"And where would I find a math geek before homeroom?" I asked myself. Without another word, I set out down the hall.

Chapter Four - Transformations

The math lab is a tiny little room near the end of the hall that leads to the library. It used to be a broom closet I think, because I can't imagine anything else that could have fit in there before they put some low shelves along the walls and set up computer workstations on them. It's cramped, smells like old socks, and there are no windows, but I guess it was the best they could do, seeing as how the only other spare room is used to store football equipment. I passed right by it as I raced down the hallway – the entrance is around a corner that leads to one of the school's emergency exits, but I stepped back when I reached the library, and spotted the handwritten sign above the door. I tried to march inside, but a bunch of kids were hanging out in the doorway, making it difficult to get by.

"Um, excuse me," I grumbled as I squeezed through and wormed my way into the room. Once inside, I scanned all around. Lots of kids were crammed in; many were typing at the computers, some standing by the printer waiting for printouts, and a few others were huddled around a short, scrawny, freckle-faced boy in dorky clothes and oversized glasses who waved his hands wildly as he spoke.

"Gerald!" I called out as I pushed my way toward him. "Gerald Hoffsteadler! You're here!" His head reflexively turned to the sound of his name, and when he spotted me, he called back, "Will? Will Allen! I know you. You're Jeannine's friend..."

"Right! That's me!" I said breathlessly as I stepped up to him. "So, where's Jeannine? Is she all right?"

"She's *great!*" Gerald said. "She's amazing! You wouldn't believe what..."

"Never mind!" I growled. At that moment, my curiosity about the previous night's events was dead. I don't know what it was – maybe that dream spooked me somehow, but all I wanted was to see Jeannine, see her alive and whole in one of her crazy outfits, her hair in some strange, inhuman color, smiling like she does just before she stomps on my foot with her steel-toed boot. "Just tell me where she is!"

"Sure! She's right over there."

"She's in *here?*" I sputtered, turning to look. It was hard to imagine how I could have missed seeing her. "Where?"

"Right over there," Gerald repeated, pointing at someone sitting at one of the computers.

Now, I could tell right off that something strange was going on, and I don't just mean the smell. You see, normally Jeannine wouldn't be caught dead in the math lab. Not because she doesn't like math, in fact, she's one of the best students in the double-accelerated math class, just like me. No, the reason you won't find either of us in that room is that being seen there is a one-way ticket to eternal geekdom. If you get spotted coming out that door, you may as well have the word NERD tattooed on your forehead and be done with it. But if Jeannine being in that room was a surprise, what I saw next was an absolute shock. Like a bolt of lightning kind of shock. I looked where Gerald was pointing and squinted a few times to be sure my eyes were working properly.

"No-No way," I gasped.

I could not believe what I was seeing. The girl Gerald pointed at was...I don't know how else to say it – *gorgeous.* Not that Jeannine hasn't always been a pretty girl, but she never...you know, *acted* pretty. She always looks more like a cross between a gypsy and a storm trooper than a society girl. She never wears make-up or girly clothes; in fact, until she wore a dress to Timmy Newsome's house the other night, I thought she didn't even own one. And at least then she wasn't in public, where everybody could see.

But the girl Gerald pointed to was wearing a fancy cream-colored satin and lace blouse tucked neatly into the waist of a teal satin skirt with soft pleats all around. She had on simple, matching jewelry: there wasn't a single gothic skull ring on any of her fingers. I scanned up and down - her hair was a single color – a rich, chocolate brown, drizzled with shimmering highlights like in a shampoo commercial. Her complexion was smooth and clear, and her skin tone was even and rosy. But the real shock was below. On her feet were real shoes, not steel-toed combat boots.

Now, none of that may sound bad to you, but it's the most _un_Jeannine-like sight I'd ever seen.

"Jeannine?" I mumbled at first, but then found my voice. "Jeannine!"

She looked up from the computer screen. Her smile was positively glowing, in part, I could see, because she was wearing blush on her cheeks.

"Oh, Hi Will!" she called out as I rushed over to her. "I was just writing about you..."

"Jeannine, are you OK?" I sputtered. I instinctively reached into my pocket for my MonsterScope to make sure this was really her, but of course it wasn't there. Instead, I looked her over, checking for...I don't know, anything monster*ish*. "What happened to you? You look so...um..."

Jeannine's eyes narrowed, and a little furrow formed in the crease between her brows.

"*Yesss?*" she said very slowly, holding the '*s*' so long that it became a hiss. Her grin was still broad, but her eyes flickered dangerously.

"So...*different*," I mumbled. "What happened? Did..."

I looked around to make sure no one was listening, then whispered, "...Did Gerald's monster do this to you?"

"No!" she gasped indignantly. "Are you saying that I look *bad*?"

"No, you look...*amazing*!" I replied quickly. "I'm just saying that this is a...well, a very big change. And the only thing that happened since I saw you last is you went to battle Gerald's monster. So naturally, I thought..."

"For your information, Will Allen," she countered, "that is not the only thing that's happened since you saw me last."

"There's more? Like what, getting struck by lightning? Because that's the only thing I can imagine would cause you to lose your mind – I mean, just look at you! What is that you're wearing?"

Jeannine looked down at her outfit, and a grin spread back across her face.

"Well, let's just say that new clothes go with

new...*ventures.*"

"What? What in the world are you talking about?"

Right then, Jeannine finally did something that made her look like the girl I knew. Her lips tightened, and she rolled her eyes at me.

"Will Allen," she said in her familiar, haughty tone. "Sometimes you can be so obtuse."

"I...I am not!" I sputtered.

Jeannine smiled slyly. "You don't know what that means, do you?"

"I know it's not something good!"

"It means you can be dense, thick headed, clueless."

"So then why didn't you just say that?! And I am *not* clueless!"

"Well, you're definitely clueless about *some* things," she giggled. "At least, that's what my blog is going to say."

"Your blog?"

Jeannine pointed at the screen she was typing on.

"I'm starting my own blog. That way I can fill everybody in on all of the interesting things that are happening."

"Would you mind," I slowly growled, "filling *me* in on all of the interesting..."

At that very moment, the warning bell for homeroom sounded.

"Oops!" Jeannine chuckled, closing her screen and quickly getting up. "I guess it will have to wait. We've got to get to homeroom!"

And then she turned and headed off. I just hissed, and followed her.

"Wait up!" I called after her, but she smiled and kept walking. But she was in those girly shoes and I was in sneakers, so naturally I caught up.

"So what happened last night? Did you find Gerald's monster, or go to a salon for a makeover instead?"

Jeannine looked back, but only for a moment.

"Oh, I found Gerald's monster," she said as we approached homeroom. "And let me tell you, it's a good thing that it was me that did it."

"What? What do you mean by that?"

"Well, let's face it Will. You're not very good at noticing important things going on around you."

"How can you say that? I'm the one who..."

But right then we arrived at our class and Jeannine whispered, "Shush!" then walked through the door. Homeroom was buzzing, at it usually does, with kids all over the place hanging out at each others desks, finishing homework that they should have done the day before, and, in the case of guys like Jacko, looking for someone to pick on. I followed Jeannine inside, and sat at the desk next to her. Leaning in, I whispered, "What do you mean it's good that it was you?"

Jeannine gave me that sly smile again, but then sighed, and whispered back, "Well, Gerald's hidden beast was a very odd monster. And really brutal...it fought like a Banshee – well, of course it did, because it *was* a Banshee. Anyway, in the end I discovered its true form, and I don't think you would have..."

"Hilmar?" the teacher's voice rang out. "Hilmar Allen?"

That's right, we're back to where my story started. So now that you're all caught up, hopefully the rest of this will make a little more sense. At least to *you*.

So anyway, after that whole disaster with the teacher calling me by my *other* name, and once Jacko got back to his seat, I turned back to Jeannine.

"So," I whispered. "What was so special about Gerald's monster that I wouldn't have..."

But Jeannine's eyes were glazed, and she didn't seem to hear me.

"Hilmar?" She choked out.

"Keep it down!" I hissed.

"*Hilmar?*"

"I was named after some old uncle or something, OK? I've kept it a secret for as long as I can remember."

"I thought you told me everything! *Hilmar!*"

"Sheesh, Jeannine! It never came up. OK? But anytime you want to know something about me, all you have to do is ask. Meanwhile, I've been trying all morning to get you to tell me about what happened to you – the monsters, your new look, and I can't even get one word from you about any of that! What's going on with you?"

"You think there's something wrong with me?" Jeannine asked defensively. "Do these clothes make me so different to you?"

"Well, no..." I mumbled. Honestly, once I had gotten over the shock of it, I had to admit that Jeannine looked good. And even though her change in style seemed very sudden, I guess I should have seen it coming, what with the flowery dress she wore to Timmy Newsome's house the other night.

"Look, I'm sorry I didn't tell you about...that name," I said. "I've never told *anyone*. I hate to even say it out loud. As soon as I get old enough, I'm changing it, and that will be the end of it."

Jeannine gave me an appraising look, and then scratched her head.

"All right, *Hilmar.*"

"*Please* don't call me that. My name is Will. Just Will."

"OK, Just-Will," she agreed. "I'll call you whatever name you want. But do you think the rest of the class will go along?"

She was right, of course. The horrible word had been released. Now it would spread through the class like a virus. It was only a matter of time before...

"Hilmar?" I heard someone to my right squeal in delight. "That's freaky. Just right for a little freak!"

I turned and saw that it was the two girls from the bus Jaime and Tiffany.

"Oh, shut up and leave him alone, Jaime!" Jeannine barked.

Jaime straightened. "Me? I'm not the one that said it…" she began, but Tiffany cut her off.

"Oooh, defending your little boyfriend, are you?" she purred at Jeannine.

"I don't need defending!" I growled at them, still fuming about how Jaime's colossal boyfriend had shoved me off the bus. "Not from anyone!"

Jaime recoiled a bit, then looked me over carefully like I was a barking dog she wasn't sure she should run away from. I aimed my glare at the other girl, but she ignored me, and faced Jeannine.

"So, I suppose now you think you're cool enough to hang with us?" she cooed.

"Cool enough to hang with you?" I injected. "Why would she join *you*? You're the ones who aren't cool enough! None of you could do what she's done!"

"Oh, you don't think our mommies could drive us to auditions too?"

"Auditions? Jeannine's done things you couldn't even dream of. You don't have the brains or the courage."

She looked at me like I was an alien, then just turned her head and muttered "just too weird," as she turned and walked away. Jaime followed, but not without a quick, backward glance at me. For some reason, her eyes fixed on me a moment, but then she quickly turned away and was gone.

Well, I just stood there with the same look of shock and confusion on my face that I had when my mother told me she'd signed me up for Yoga classes. I turned to Jeannine, and she had a bemused look on her face.

"So, does *everybody* know something I don't?" I grumbled.

Jeannine giggled.

"I guess so," she said. "Quite a turn for little Jimmy Neutron, boy genius, isn't it?"

"You know I hate when people call me that!" I growled, but that just seemed to amuse her even more. My cheeks started heating up like a blast furnace, but she just giggled.

"Would you please," I grumbled through gritted teeth, "just tell me what all this is about?"

Jeannine was still smiling, clearly enjoying my moment of confusion, but finally, she relented.

"Well," she said. "You know that audition my mom took me to the other day?"

"Of course," I mumbled.

"Well," she went on, "As it turns out, I got a call back. This morning before school they brought me in for a second audition for a major role in 'The Ugly Stepsister's Lament'."

"The what?" I sputtered.

"'The Ugly Stepsister's Lament'," she repeated. "It's this famous book that's being made into a movie. They're shooting here in town, and that's what I auditioned for."

"And?" I asked, though the answer was obvious.

"And..." She paused for effect, like a true drama queen. "...And I got it! The director said I gave a remarkably brave performance; that I stood out head and shoulders above everyone else! I'm going to be in a movie! A real movie!"

"So that explains why you're...eh, *in costume?*"

Jeannine giggled, and looked down at her outfit.

"Oh, I don't know. I kind of like it," she said. "It looks very classy."

"It looks very *'I work at a bank'*. What happened to your whole *I'm a Bohemian* thing?"

"Underneath all this, I'm still like my grandmother," Jeannine insisted. "But Agatha Cromwell isn't."

"Who?"

"Agatha Cromwell," Jeannine explained. "That's who

I'm going to be in the movie. And a good actress has to immerse herself in her role, so for now, this is how I'll dress. Well, at least until Gym."

"Well, I guess it's OK," I grumbled, but then added cheerfully, "So this is pretty cool then! Now you can be an accomplished actress on top of being a successful...you know."

Strangely, now that I showed some enthusiasm, a bit of her own faded.

"Um, yes. About that..."

"What?"

But just then, the bell sounded, and we had to go to class.

"Um, I'll tell you about it at lunch," she said, and then got right up and left me sitting there with my mouth hanging open stupidly.

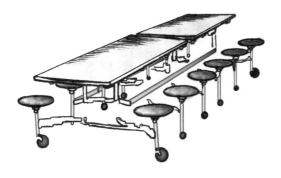

Chapter Five - Spills

Classes that morning seemed to drag on forever. The seconds hand on the clock spun in slow motion as I waited for the lunch period to arrive, and I fidgeted impatiently for long stretches of time.

Unfortunately, that did not go unnoticed.

"Are we keeping you from something, Mr. Allen?" my Math teacher, Mrs. McAllister droned. My eyes, which had been drifting lazily, spun forward to find her hovering over me (again) with her hawkish black eyes fixed on me like I was a prairie dog scurrying for a burrow. I bolted straight up in my seat faster than you can say 'detention'. Or, more importantly, faster than Mrs. McAllister can say it.

"No, ma'am. Of course not." I lied. I don't think that she bought it though, and Mrs. McAllister isn't the tolerant, forgiving sort. She pursed her lips, and adjusted her thick, horn-rimmed glasses.

"Perhaps you need more to amuse yourself with?" she said sharply, just as she always does before she punishes me with three thousand extra equations to solve. "Let's see if you…"

"Excuse me, Mrs. McAllister?" Jeannine called out from her seat across the room. Jeannine and I used to sit together in that class, but Mrs. McAllister moved me to a seat on the opposite end of the room back in early October. Fortunately though, even though she treats me like I'm a splinter under her fingernail, Mrs. McAllister has a soft spot for Jeannine.

"Yes, Miss Fitsimmons?" Mrs. McAllister replied. Her tone instantly turned much softer. "What is it, dear?"

"Um, I'm having a little trouble with exercise 17," Jeannine answered. "Is it possible to go over it on the board?"

"Of course, dear," Mrs. McAllister said. She didn't say '*Anything for my favorite student*,' but she might just as well have. As Mrs. McAllister returned to the front of the class, I looked at Jeannine, and she shot me a wink. I silently mouthed the words '*thank you*' to her, and she smiled, and then went back to work.

The rest of that morning's classes were uneventful, except for Mr. Munson's science class, where we dissected earthworms. It was really gross, and the smell was disgusting, but I probably shouldn't have said so out loud. Mr. Munson, a tall, gray, pudgy man with a bad comb-over, is a good and decent teacher, and he likes me a lot more than Mrs. McAllister, but not so much that he didn't make me clean up all the trays after class. Because of that, I was late getting to lunch, and Jeannine was already seated at our table when I came through the door.

"Thanks for bailing me out in Math," I said as I sat down next to her. Jeannine smiled.

"It was no big deal," she replied. "Keeping you out of trouble seems to be my job these days, doesn't it?" I looked down, a little ashamed of myself.

"Yeah, um…" I muttered. "Look, I'm sorry if I gave you a hard time about your new look and all."

"Well, it *was* something of a shock, wasn't it?

"Yeah. But really, I think it was because I got all worked up worrying about you facing the…*you know what* without me. I should have known better. I knew you could do it."

"I sure could! You should have seen it, Will! Gerald's monster grew so big that his room…"

"SHHHHH!" I hissed. "Jeannine! Be quiet!"

"Oh come on, Will! You complained that you've been waiting all morning for me to tell you about Gerald's monster, and now that I'm finally telling you, you don't want to hear?"

"It's not that! But do you really think we should talk about this here in the lunchroom? With a gazillion people all around us? I thought we were keeping our business a secret?"

"Oh, be serious," Jeannine replied. ""Who would actually listen to us? And with all the noise in the cafeteria, who could hear us even if they tried? I can barely hear you, and I'm...like, maybe six inches away."

I looked around the lunch room at all the faces and bodies moving about. No one seemed to notice we even existed. Then I tried listening in on the conversation of the kids sitting closest to us, but it just sounded like gibberish to me.

"OK," I finally agreed. "So then go on. How did you solve the case?"

"Oh, it was so amazing!" she squealed.

"Well," I said impatiently, "Tell me everything!"

Well, saying *that* was a big mistake. See, I should tell you – *warn* you, really: Jeannine is a good and loyal friend, and a brilliant and brave detective, but she doesn't know how to tell a story. At least not a *short* story. She droned on and on, reciting endless details about stuff I didn't really care to know about, including what Gerald's house looked like, the smell of the pizza she figured they had for dinner; his mother's clothes, their home furnishings, and even how many dirty socks were piled in the corner of his room. After what seemed like hours I finally blurted, "So when are you going to actually tell me about the monster?"

"I'm getting to that!" she said irritably, as though I was spoiling her story by asking. When Jeannine gets on a roll like that, you may as well just get comfortable or pull out a book to read, because there's no interrupting her until she's done. She becomes kind of like a charging bull, but for the unpleasant smell.

Of course, I meant the *bull* smells bad, not Jeannine.

"So," Jeannine continued without stopping to draw a breath (I still can't figure how she does that), "There we were..."

Just then, a commotion erupted at the cafeteria door right behind us.

"Jeannine! Hey Jeannine!" a squeaky, shrill voice called out. Jeannine sighed, and put her head in her hands.

I turned and looked at the door, but there were so many people mulling around that I couldn't spot who was talking. It was one of those moments that I definitely wished I had X-ray vision.

"What's all that?" I wondered out loud.

Jeannine sighed.

"Maybe I did my job a little too well," she whispered.

"You solved the case," I said proudly. "You conquered the monster. So what could be wrong?"

"It's Gerald," she groaned. "He's been following me around all morning..."

Just then, Gerald's shrill voice cut through the air again.

"Jeannine! Wait there! I'm getting my lunch!"

Jeannine glowered. "As if it's not enough that I saved him from his monster, now he wants me to be friends with him too."

"Well of course," I snickered. "After all, you're his hero! He probably doodles pictures of you wearing a Supergirl costume in his notebook."

"It's not funny, Will! I could use some help here!"

"What, because now he thinks you're the greatest thing since sliced bread? What's the problem with that?"

"The problem is, Gerald has been following me around like a lost puppy all day," she said grimly. "So I thought, maybe I could bring him around to hang out with *you* at lunch today. You could, you know, be his pal. That way he won't need to bother me all the time."

I looked at her like she was speaking Swahili.

"If he hangs out with me," I asked, "won't that mean he'll be hanging out with *you* too, seeing as how we're here together?"

Jeannine looked away uncomfortably, and began picking lint off of her skirt.

"Actually," she said, "I was thinking of sitting with Timmy Newsome today."

She looked back at me nervously, and then before my mouth could even drop open, she began rattling off her excuse at lightning speed.

"See, even though his monster is gone, Timmy is still having trouble dealing with his dad's...you know...*girlfriend*, so I've been talking him through it, since I've been there myself," she said breathlessly. "And, well...we got to talking about other stuff too, and then he asked if I would come sit with him during lunch today, and..."

"So is this, like, a first date or something?" I interrupted. "Is that why Timmy can't just come over here and sit with *us*? Because if you're asking me to hang out with Gerald so that you..."

"It's not like that!" Jeannine shot back angrily. But then she gave me a funny look and added, "Anyway, what if it was? You don't have a problem with me being with Timmy, do you?"

"No!" I spat instantly. "But that doesn't mean I'm going to babysit Gerald The 'Lost Puppy' Hoffsteadtler for you! How do I even know he's housebroken?"

"Oh, come on Will!" she growled. "You'll like hanging out with Gerald. On top of everything else you two have in common, he's a baseball fan just like you. You'll probably have lots to talk about."

"I can be perfectly happy sitting by myself for lunch thank you very much," I snarled. "Why can't Gerald just sit with you and Timmy?"

"Oh, Gerald would never want to sit at that table," Jeannine stated flatly. "Timmy's the football team's manager, so he sits at the jocks' table."

"Manager?" I quipped. "What does he manage? Their jockstraps?"

Jeannine's eyes narrowed, but then she took a deep breath and sighed.

"Just do me this favor so that I can have lunch with Timmy in peace," She urged. "*Pleeeeeaase*?"

And then she gave her best puppy-dog pout. I knew she was using it to get me to do what she wanted, but it still worked, as always.

"Oh, all right," I muttered in defeat.

"Great!" Jeannine cheered, suddenly spry and bouncy again. "I knew I could count on you, Will."

As if on cue, Gerald finally returned from getting his lunch and marched on up to us.

"Hi Jeannine!" He said brightly. "...and uh, Will."

I frowned at Jeannine, but she quickly shot me a *you promised* kind of look, and I rolled my eyes, but then gave in.

"Hi Gerald," I said flatly, moving over to make room. "Why don't you come sit with us?"

Let me tell you, Gerald was in that seat faster than my mom can burn pancakes. He squeezed in between me and Jeannine and faced her, leaving me to look at the back of his head.

"Yow!" I howled as I slid over onto the sharp part of the broken seat. But no one seemed to notice.

"So," Gerald said. "Do you two always..."

But Jeannine wasted no time. "Excuse me, Gerald," she interrupted. "I've got to take care of something for a few minutes. Why don't you hang out here until I get back? I'm sure you and Will have a lot to talk about. He's my partner, so you can fill him in about…our little adventure."

"Oh, I…OK," Gerald mumbled, but Jeannine had already gotten up and taken her lunch bag with her. She walked over to the other side of the lunch room, and both Gerald and I watched her go. Finally, Gerald turned to me awkwardly and said, "Her partner, huh?"

"Yeah," I mumbled irritably, still rubbing my stinging…um, *thigh* where the seat had scratched me. But then I saw Gerald watching me, and quickly put my hand in my pocket instead.

"Well, that explains a lot," he said.

"Yeah."

We stared at each other for a few seconds, and then without another word we opened our lunch bags and began eating. Actually, I wouldn't exactly call what Gerald was doing *eating*. The sounds of his grunts and growls made me look over at him, and if I didn't know better, I'd have thought Jeannine missed at least one of his monsters, because it looked like Gerald's peanut butter and jelly sandwich was attacking his face. And winning. The peanut butter had found a stronghold upon Gerald's chin, cheeks, and nose, and jelly was dripping everywhere. I was disgusted, and for once it wasn't because my mom had given me turnip custard. Gerald must have sensed that I was staring at him – he looked up from his sandwich and mumbled through his full mouth, "*Whaf? Ith somefin wong?*" Bits fell out when he spoke, and I just couldn't take it.

"Um, nothing," I muttered. "I just gotta…go to the bathroom. See ya."

And I got up and walked a few steps before I remembered that I left my lunch on the table. I turned back, but suddenly, I got a…I don't know – *antsy* feeling.

Now, Jeannine may say that I don't notice things going on around me, but I could feel something bad was coming. The hairs on the back of my neck stood on end, and I began turning my head, searching the cafeteria for anything suspicious.

"*Wiwll?*" Gerald said, making me turn back to him. "*Awe you OK?*"

But I had already begun wandering blindly as my eyes continued to scan the room looking for dark, mysterious, dangers. The problem with that is sometimes the threats someone like me or Gerald face aren't dark enough or mysterious enough to stand out in a crowded middle school lunch room. As I stood there, checking out all corners of the room, a couple of boys in team jackets passed behind me as they strutted toward the lunch line. They slowed as they passed Gerald, and I realized that they were pulling something from inside their jackets a moment too late.

"Bonzai!" one of the jacketed boys cried out, just as they dumped something slimy and green all over Gerald, and then ran off. But they didn't run far. They stopped when they reached the jock's table, and then patted a few of their friends' shoulders and pointed at Gerald. Laughing broke out – nasty, mean-spirited laughs. People stopped on their way to their seats and pointed – some even came in for a closer look. Gerald just sat there covered in green goop, alone and miserable, feeling the weight of everyone's laughter crushing down on him like a two ton boulder on his shoulders. I'm ashamed to admit that my first thought was that I was glad it wasn't me. I was too stunned to think of anything to do – I looked around for some teachers or something, but they were nowhere to be seen.

"Hey, want some gravy to go with that?" someone called out, which brought on another roar of laughter.

My blood began to boil, and my cheeks flushed.

""Stop it!" I cried out, rushing forward, pushing through the circle of kids that had surrounded Gerald. "Leave him alone!"

I squirmed and shoved until I was at Gerald's side. He was just sitting there, not moving, not yelling, not even crying. He was just…*sitting* there, covered in goop.

"Come on, Gerald," I said, grabbing his arm and lifting him up, "Let's go. You gotta…you gotta get cleaned up…"

But even though I pulled and tugged, he wouldn't get up. He just sat there, as stiff as my mother's oatmeal. Except that my mother's oatmeal isn't covered in green slime.

It's purple.

Anyway, there I was tugging on Gerald when some of the boys from the jock's table pushed through the crowd to admire their work.

"Whoa, you landed that one right on target! Good job, guys!"

"Yah mon! He be lookin' like a ice cream sundae!"

"Duh huh! Makes him look better, if ya ask me!"

"Hey look! Doofus Dorkenstein is helpin' his buddy out! We got any slime leftover for him?"

I recognized the last voice. It was Jacko McNulty. I looked up to see him gleefully taking a goop-crusted plastic bag from under the jacket of one of his buddies. Now, it doesn't take a master detective to figure out what was coming next. But as Jacko carefully turned toward me with the bag, I rushed up, grabbed the bottom of the bag, and squeezed. The green goop came shooting out the top, spraying all over Jacko. Some of it splattered on me too, but it was worth it. The look of shock on Jacko's face as the glop splashed him in the mouth was priceless.

Well, *almost* priceless. Seeing as how Jacko's look of shock was quickly replaced by a look of rage, it was pretty clear that the price for that little move was about to go up like umbrellas in a rainstorm.

"You…you…" he sputtered, with goop coming out of his mouth as he spoke, "That's *two* I owe you now."

He grabbed my by the shirt, but I spun out of his grasp. Unfortunately, I was surrounded by Jacko's jock buddies, so every direction I turned was blocked by some team-jacketed goon. Suddenly, something heavy fell upon my shoulders, and squeezed them with a vise-like grip. I turned my head, and saw something big hanging over me. Well, actually, it was more of a some*one*. A big, tall, wide someone: that rhino-size jock from the bus – who had apparently had grown even more enormous since the morning, or at least it seemed that way now that his huge head was looming right over mine. Jacko smiled an evil smirk as he slowly advanced on me, while I squirmed desperately to get free.

"What, no smart words now, you freakin'geek?" Jacko hissed as he leaned toward me.

"Why waste any on you? You're too stupid to understand them."

Now, I'd love to take credit for that remark. It's the kind of quick, witty retort I wish I had come up with. But it wasn't me. That clever insult came from a familiar, haughty-sounding girl's voice just outside the wall of jocks. At that very moment, Jeannine pushed her way in through the crowd, with Timmy right behind her. She stepped right in front of me and stood there between me and Jacko. Jacko straightened, and sized her up.

"What do *you* want?" he spat.

"World peace," she replied.

"Let him go, Truck," Timmy said to the hulk that was holding tight to my shoulders. The big ape just ignored him. Timmy spun furiously at Jacko. "Let him go!"

"You ain't in charge here, Timmy-boy," Jacko hissed. "You're nothin'. You're just a freakin' errand boy."

Jeannine turned, and before anyone could react, she slapped Truck, if that's really what the big oaf's name was, and shoved his hands from my shoulders. Truck fell back, mostly from shock I think, but Jacko's eyes grew wide as Jeannine rounded on him once more.

"Oooh, tough girl!" he snickered.

Jeannine stepped right up to his face and said, "Come on, then. Show us how tough *you* are."

Jacko held still a moment, but then looked at Jeannine, and then back over her shoulder at me.

No, actually it *wasn't* me, but something else that caught his eye. It must have been something tall by the look of it, because he was staring right over the top of my head. Anyway, I wasn't taking my eye off of Jacko so I don't know what he saw, but he suddenly straightened up.

"Hey, Dunk!" he chuckled. "Check this out! You think coach sent Timmy here to clean up our smelly mess again?"

Timmy glared at him.

"No," Timmy growled, and then turned and looked back over my head too. "And if I were you, Dunk, I'd keep from making any more messes. I don't think coach was too happy about the last one."

Jacko chuckled nastily, but then glanced up over my head again and said, "What?"

"Not here, Jacko," a deep, commanding voice replied from right behind me.

"This runt messed up my jacket, Dunk!"

"Later," the voice warned. "Timmy is right. Coach will go crazy if we get into any more trouble."

I don't know what any of that was about, but Jacko suddenly backed off. I finally looked back to see who he was answering to, and standing there beside Truck was a shorter, thinner, and yet far more impressive figure - our school's star athlete, Duncan Williams. I knew who he was because his picture has been posted on every wall and in every school newspaper since I first came to Ashford. Sometimes I've even seen him in the pages of my dad's newspaper when he holds it up between us at breakfast, and it's always followed by some story, "Duncan Williams Wins *This*," or "Duncan Williams Sets New Record In *That*." Jeannine looked over at him too, and cringed.

No, not cringed – *swooned* is more like it. And it was easy to see why. This guy looked like a golden statue that had sprung down from the top of an Olympic Trophy. He stood perfectly straight and tall, and even with his team jacket on you could see strong, lean muscles flexing through his athletic-cut polo shirt. His polished, darkly-tanned face was the kind you see on the covers of magazines - kind of a cross between Alex Rodriguez and Justin Bieber, and his perfectly combed hair was jet black, wavy, and all shimmery. His clothes were as clean and crisp as a fashion model's, and even his fingernails shined. Everyone seemed to be affected by his presence, even Jacko, who stepped back, but then, as if he had changed his mind, straightened up fiercely.

"You don't tell me what to do!" he challenged. "That kid messed with me! Truck, tell him!"

"Duh...yeah. The kid needs to learn his place," Truck agreed.

"We'll teach him his place," Dunk said, giving me a nasty, sideways leer that was scarier than Jacko's look of wide-eyed rage. "But not now. Remember what Coach Jenner said? If there's trouble again, someone's getting suspended for sure."

Jacko looked around and, as if noticing the crowd for the first time, suddenly looked uneasy.

"All right, all right," he finally agreed. But before he melted back into the crowd, he pointed his finger at me and hissed, "But this ain't over, Dorkenstein." And then he was gone. The rest of them soon followed, and the crowd began to break up. I walked over to Timmy.

"Thanks, Timmy," I said. Timmy nodded.

"I guess we're even," he said. I smiled and said, "Now I owe *you* a chocolate bar." Then I turned to Jeannine.

"Thanks," I said. She beamed at me and replied, "You're welcome. After all, what are partners for?"

Just then, a shrill voice called out, "Jeannine! Hey, Jeannine!" Jeannine cringed, and muttered, "Outta here!" as she quickly grabbed Timmy by the wrist and hurried away. Gerald stepped on up and asked, "Where is she going?" I looked back at him, still covered in goop, and replied, "Um…bathroom. She does that a lot. It's a girl thing." Gerald looked over to where Jeannine had disappeared into the crowd, and then back at me.

"Thanks Will. Thanks for standing up for me."

I squirmed. I don't know why, but I was as uncomfortable with Gerald's gratitude as Jeannine had been.

"It…it was nothing," I mumbled.

But Gerald couldn't let it go.

"No one ever stood up for me before," he gushed.

"Well, maybe if you show some backbone," I growled, "People wouldn't give you so much trouble."

Gerald just looked away and pouted.

"You…you don't like me either," he said quietly.

"What? I…I don't even know you…"

Gerald didn't seem to hear me.

"Even people like you and Jeannine. Even people who act nice to me don't really want me around. Nobody does."

"Look…" I tried to say, but Gerald seemed to be lost in his own misery.

"Everyone hates me," he muttered to himself.

Well, now I just felt about two inches high.

"Nobody hates you, Gerald, it's just...it's just that..."

"What?"

"It's just people don't like it when you cling to them and stuff. It puts them off."

"I just want them to be my friends."

"I know. Just...back off a little, you know? Don't act so needy."

Gerald straightened up and put his hand to his chin, like he was figuring out a tough math problem.

"So let me get this straight," he pondered. "The best way to make friends is to act like I don't need any?"

"Well, I wouldn't put it that way..."

"Is that what worked for you?"

"Huh?" I mumbled, suddenly confused. "What do you mean?"

"Well, how did you get Jeannine to be friends with you?"

"Well, I...I didn't *get* her to be friends with me," I stammered awkwardly. "That's just what we are. That's how we've always been."

For some reason, Gerald suddenly glared at me.

"You make it sound so easy!" he said heatedly. "You just don't know what it's like, coming here every day, and nobody likes you. Getting teased and bullied all the time – it's horrible."

I squirmed, because I knew exactly how he felt. In fact, at that moment his feelings seemed to pass through the air like vapor, and I could almost ...well, *smell* them.

Maybe Jeannine was right about me and Gerald after all, I thought. *Maybe we **are** alike.*

I looked back at him sympathetically, just in time to watch him wipe a booger onto his sleeve. Well, *mostly* onto his sleeve.

*Then again, we're definitely not **that** much alike.*

"Look," I finally said. "You conquered *monsters*. After

that, how bad could going to school be?"

Gerald looked back at the jocks' table, and his eyes seemed to alight with flame.

"Some things," he growled, "are even worse than monsters."

"If you defeated your monsters," I insisted, "you can handle whatever else comes your way."

"That doesn't change anything," Gerald maintained. "Even without the monsters, today is the same as yesterday. More school. More bullies. And no friends."

That last bit finally did it. I threw up my hands and shouted, "All right, all right! You want friends? I'll be your friend, OK?"

"Really?"

"Really! Now go clean yourself up! You look like broccoli with syrup on top! And *not* in a good way!"

"Sure! Anything you say, *friend*!"

And with that he turned and walked off, smiling broadly.

"Brilliant," I grumbled. "Why didn't I think of that before?"

As I stood there watching my new booger and slime covered friend head out of the lunchroom, the warning bell sounded.

"Oh, great!" I growled. "I didn't even get to eat anything yet!" And I quickly grabbed my lunch bag and opened it. Inside was a... well whatever it had been, it was now a scrunched, smushed, brownish blob between slime-covered bread.

"Ugh! That green goop looked more appetizing," I whispered to myself. But I was hungry, so I quickly peeled off of the wax paper my mom had wrapped it in and pulled the sandwich from the bag. As if on cue, some of the slime that had splashed on me when I squirted Jacko dripped off of my shoulder right onto the sandwich. I stared at the goop-covered bread for a moment, deciding whether to hazard biting into it anyway. As I stood there thinking it over, more goop dripped down, this time from my hair, and began seeping down the front of my shirt. The sight of my goop-covered clothes made me think of Gerald, covered in slime and boogers, and I sort of lost my appetite. I dumped my sandwich and headed to the bathroom instead.

You know, when a day starts going downhill, it can turn from bad to awful in a hurry. A quick check in the boy's room mirror revealed that I had a lot more of that goop on me than I thought, and as it turned out, there were no paper towels left. So the next thing you know, there I was, wiping green goop off my head with toilet paper, when things turned even worse. Like, asteroids falling from the sky worse.

"Hello, Dorkenstein," called out a smarmy, oily voice that echoed around the hollow, empty walls of the bathroom.

Chapter Six - Directions

"Well, lookie here, boys!" snarled the voice. I looked up from the sink and saw Jacko McNulty's ugly face sneering at me in the mirror. I cursed myself silently, thinking I should have heard...or at least, *smelled* him coming, but I guess his odor blended in perfectly with the usual stench of the bathroom (this being middle school, you'd think guys would have learned to flush the toilet by now). As I stared at him in the mirror, his awkward, herky-jerky twitches made it look like he was getting slapped on the back of his head by an invisible hand. Or maybe that was just wishful thinking. My eyes quickly sought out the exit, but it was already too late. Jacko's buddy, Truck, stood leaning up against the door, pounding his fist into his hand. Just then, two more large, team-jacketed figures emerged from the stalls, and I was instantly surrounded. One was like a smaller version of Truck, with a darker crew cut but the same wide build and flat face, while the other, who wore a knit cap with a Jamaican flag on the front, was tall and stringy with dark skin, long black curls, and more gold chains hanging around his neck than a disco queen.

Now just so you know, in the past week alone I've found myself under attack by flying fanged jaws, spears of flame, a man-eating toilet, a flying shark, and a shrieking harpy, and I had only a flashlight to defend myself with. Even so, I don't think I've ever felt more trapped than the moment I looked up into the boy's room mirror and saw that I was alone with a bunch of freakishly large jocks, each of whom wore an evil grin that could do that harpy proud.

"So, did you think you were going to get away with it?" a deep voice hissed. I turned, and over by the window stood Duncan Williams, his golden-boy face twisted into a menacing scowl. His perfect complexion, polished hair, and sleek jacket glittered in the light pouring in from the window, and I thought to myself that villains aren't supposed to look so good.

"Get away with what?" I barked back.

"Nobody messes with my team, you little runt!" he crowed as he marched forward. "Nobody!"

But before Dunk ever reached me, Jacko crossed in front of him. He snapped his fingers, and the jocks behind me, mini-Truck and the Jamaican, stepped up and grabbed my shoulders. Jacko slouched toward me and leaned in until his greasy hair brushed against my nose.

"Nobody messes with *me*, Dorkenstein. Or should I call you *Hilmar*?"

"It's Will!" I shouted back as I struggled to break free. "Will Allen! Get it right, sleazeball!"

Jacko snickered, and started rolling up his sleeves, but all of a sudden, Dunk reached from behind him, put his hand on Jacko's shoulder, and pulled him around.

"Will Allen?" Dunk stuttered. *"This...*is Will Allen?"

"Yeah!" Jacko snarled, pulling himself free. "So?"

Dunk looked back at him blankly, but then backed off.

"Ah, nothing," Dunk said, though his eyes were suddenly open as wide as the crack in the Titanic. He began scratching the side of his head, but then ran his fingers back and forth, smoothing his hair. "I just thought he was...someone else."

"So what?" Jacko hissed, turning on Dunk and sneering, "You wanna send him flowers or somethin'?"

Dunk's eyes narrowed to slits, and the corners of his mouth pulled back to let out a low growl. He stared down at Jacko.

"I just thought we should get the name right," he said, his voice a soft, menacing rumble, "for the tombstone."

Dunk tilted his head in my direction, and even though I'm a fearless monster detective and all that, I felt a shiver go down my spine. Jacko's scowl turned into a broad smirk faster than you can say *dead meat.* He backed away from Dunk, and turned toward me instead.

"So, what should we start with, Rexie?" Jacko asked gleefully.

"Yo, mon. Howsa 'bout we hang him out da widow by hees ankles?" answered the Jamaican as he held tight to my left arm. I looked back at him briefly, and his nasty smile revealed a gleaming gold tooth that matched the gold chains around his neck. I looked over at Mini-Truck, but he just grinned, and blew a bubbled with the gum he was chewing. Jacko let out a nasty chuckle, and then from all across the room, his teammates eagerly threw out more of their most inspired suggestions.

"Major League Wedgie?"

"Swirlie!"

"Tape him to a toilet!"

Charming, huh? But then jocks aren't exactly known for cleverness and creativity, are they? But if most of the group seemed to grow more excited at each new idea, at least one of them was unsatisfied.

"No, wait," Dunk cut in. "I'm tired of the same old stuff all the time. I think we should do something special with this one."

"Oooh, me like!" the Jamaican howled in delight.

"Well, you *are* the team captain," Jacko agreed, although his voice sounded resentful. "Whatta you got in mind?"

Dunk turned toward me. His face was twisted into an evil leer, but an awkward one, because his eyes remained wide, almost like they refused to go along.

"First, you're going to clean off Trevor's jacket for him..."

"Who's Trevor?"

Dunk blinked, and looked at me like I had grown horns.

"Are you dense?" Dunk spat. He quickly turned and pointed at Jacko. "Trevor McNulty, all-county halfback two years running! I thought you knew who you were dealing with."

He pointed again and said, "You're going to clean off his jacket..."

"You're Trevor?" I said to Jacko.

"You're Hilmar?" he crowed back.

"Hmmm. Good point." I muttered.

"You're going to clean his jacket," Dunk repeated impatiently, "You're going to clean it with your bare hands. You're going to make it spotless. Then you're going to put that jacket back on him, nice and neat. And once everything is back like it should be, we're all going to stand you up in front of Trevor and then..."

Dunk's teammates were leaning in, eager to hear what horror he had in mind. I have to admit, I cringed a bit as he spoke.

"And then..." he paused, and I held my breath. "...Then you're going to apologize."

I blinked, and looked up, thinking it must be a joke or something. Apparently, I wasn't the only one who thought so. Dunk's friends leaned back and looked at him like he had just put on a dress.

"What?" whined Jacko, or Trevor, or whatever his name was. His mammoth friend, Truck, twitched, and tilted his huge head.

"Duh, Dunk, really...?"

"It's perfect," Dunk insisted. "We work the kid like an old cleaning lady, and then make him apologize. He makes amends and learns not to mess with us. And we don't get suspended by coach for getting into trouble."

His buddies still seemed too stunned for words.

"No hanging him by his ankles?" mini-Truck grumbled. "No swirlie?"

"What for? He's already a mess – he's got slime all over him and toilet paper stuck in his hair. We'd only be helping him clean up."

A few of the boys nodded, but...

"No freakin' way!" Jacko spat. "This kid's got it coming, and we're gonna give it to him! Right, Truck?"

"Duhhh..." Truck sputtered, as though no one had ever asked him to speak before. "Well, uh...we should do *something*..."

"Freakin' right!" shouted Jacko, pointing at Truck and nodding his head. He turned back to Dunk and glared at him fiercely. "Freakin' right! Truck knows what's what! And we ain't gonna let this kid get off with just some crummy little 'I'm sorry'!"

Dunk stared back coldly, but when he replied it wasn't Jacko he spoke to.

"Is that what *you* think, Truck?" Dunk said, his eyes still shooting lasers at Jacko.

"Um, w-well..." Truck stuttered. For someone so frighteningly large, his voice had suddenly shrunk to that of a mouse.

"Who's the man, Truck?" Dunk hissed. "Who's the one who gets it done?"

"You're the man, Dunk, but..."

"So, are you with me?"

"I...uh..."

At just that moment, the door to the bathroom opened, and in walked my science teacher, Mr. Munson. He looked up at the lot of us and froze in his tracks. All the boys suddenly straightened up, and the two holding my arms quickly dropped their grip. Mini-truck's gum bubble suddenly burst all over his face, while the Jamaican took an interest in brushing off his sleeves. Mr. Munson seemed at a loss for a moment, but then leaned his head back, cleared his throat, and spoke quite loudly.

"What is going on in here? Shouldn't all of you boys be on your way to class?"

Um, yes sir," Dunk mumbled, combing his hair with his fingers while the rest of the boys fidgeted. "We were just, ah..."

"We were just leaving," I finished for him, and then fixed my eyes on Jacko. "We're done here, aren't we?"

Jacko glared as I smirked at him viciously.

"Yeah," he grumbled. His head rocked around like a boat in a hurricane. "Yeah, we're done."

"I should think so, Mr. McNulty," Mr. Munson said, gazing over at Jacko knowingly. "I believe you are already on probation. One would certainly hope you are not engaging in behavior that would result in further disciplinary action. Your team would certainly suffer in your absence if you were to be suspended."

Jacko just looked down. "Yes sir," he finally hissed, his

head twitching even more violently. Then, head still facing down, he scampered to the door and out into the hallway. Mr. Munson's eyes followed him out the door, then he turned back to the rest of us.

"Are you quite all right, Mr. Allen?" he asked.

"Fine sir," I answered, checking out the sour faces on the huge beasts surrounding me with a big smile on my face. I felt a lot stronger with a teacher there to back me up – and now that I had an ace to play. "Everything is just fine."

Mr. Munson nodded, but then he turned his sights on Dunk and the others.

"As for the rest of you, I remind you that it is a great privilege to play for your school team. Bring us honor and you will rightfully bask in our adulation. But if you bring us shame," he looked directly at Dunk, "you will suffer to be disgraced and forgotten. Think well on that, gentlemen."

And with that, he turned and walked out. I stood there stunned for a moment. Mr. Munson had gone and left me alone again with four huge guys who would like nothing better than to send me bungee jumping – without a cord. I guess he felt confident that his words had instantly and magically brought those boys back from the dark side. Crazy, I know, but teachers can be sort of funny that way. Of course, there was a slight chance that it might have worked, but there was only one way to find out. I took a deep breath, held it, and then started walking toward the door. No one moved to stop me. I made it to the door untouched, but that big oaf, Truck, moved between me and the exit.

Now like I said before, this guy was huge. His friends may have called him 'Truck', but to me he looked more like a freight train. He stood there, not moving an inch, glaring down at me like I was a worm that ought to be mashed between the cleats of his shoes. I looked up at that big, flat face and cleared my throat.

"Excuse me," I said, staring right up at him, "Coming through here."

Truck growled, but his eyes twitched. He looked over at Dunk, and I don't know what Truck saw because I wasn't taking my eyes off him for a second, but he nodded, and then stepped aside. I kept my eyes fixed on him as I stepped past, opened the door, and marched out into the hallway. Once outside, I exhaled. Loudly.

"Whew!" I muttered. "Give me sharks and harpies over that any day."

Maybe I would have cheered – even danced a fandango, but for the fact that Truck and the others followed me out. I didn't like the idea of them walking behind me, unseen, so I backed up to the wall and stood there watching them go by as they made their way down the hallway. They all gave me dirty looks as they passed, but spoke not a word. Finally, they reached the end of the corridor, turned the corner, and disappeared from sight. I stood there for a moment, but then hurried down the hallway myself, hoping that my English Teacher, Mr. Klein, hadn't started collecting homework already. But when I turned the corner, two big, team-jacketed figures stood directly in my path.

"Well," I grumbled. "It's the Dunk and Jacko Show, part three. You know, you guys really shouldn't follow me around so much. People will talk."

And then I put my head down and continued marching down the hallway, but Jacko cut me off. He thrust his arm out across my path, blocking my way.

"What, you think you'd get off that easy?" he hissed. "I don't think so."

Now, let me be real clear about one thing: this guy did not scare me. I mean, I *was* afraid of him once, but I got over it. That's how I became a monster detective – by conquering my fears. But I'm not stupid, either.

Well actually, maybe I *am* a little stupid sometimes, especially when I get my dander up, like I did right then. Even though this guy was much bigger than me and backed up by an even bigger and stronger partner, I egged him on.

"You don't *think* at all," I spat. "Didn't you hear what Mr. Munson said? You're on probation!?"

"So what, Dorkenstein? You think I care?"

"You would if you weren't as stupid as you look. One word, genius – suspension. You hassle me any more, and you can bet that'll be the end of your season." And with that I shoved his arms out of my way. Jacko growled, and grabbed me with both hands. I reached up and took hold of one of his arms as he pulled me toward him, but before anything else happened, rescue came from a surprising source.

"Whoa, hold on, Jacko," Dunk said as he broke in between us. "The kid's right - you're on probation. You heard what the teacher said. You get into another fight and you'll be suspended."

"Good thinking," I growled at him. "What are you, his spare brain? He obviously needs one to keep from tripping over himself when he walks."

Jacko lurched at me again, but Dunk held him back.

"Don't do it," he urged. "We need you out there on the field. You don't want to blow our whole season over some wimpy little runt with a big mouth."

Jacko pushed and strained against the arms holding him back.

"C'mon, he's not worth it," Dunk said.

Jacko glared at him, but then finally backed down. He pulled himself out of Dunk's grasp, and then shook himself, and straightened his goop-covered jacket. But he turned and spat at me before he headed away.

"When the season is over," he growled, "You're freakin' dead meat."

And then he headed down the hallway. Just before he turned the next corner, Jacko looked back and saw that Dunk was still standing in front of me. He leaned back and called out, "Hey, Dunk! You coming or what?"

"Give me a second," Dunk said. Once Jacko disappeared around the corner, Dunk looked up and down the hallway to make sure no one else was still around. He began scratching his head, but when he turned back to me and saw me watching, he stopped and brushed back his hair. Then he shuffled uncomfortably in my direction.

Now, this guy wasn't a human mountain like his friend Truck, but he was no lightweight, either. Strangely though, even though he was about twice my size, when he approached me his face looked ashen, like *he* was the one who was about to get beat up. His eyes darted around like he couldn't bear to look at me. He rubbed his knuckles together, but his movements seemed more nervous than menacing. And he kept coming closer until I could smell the hamburger on his breath.

"Meet me after school outside the locker room," he finally muttered while looking over at the posters on the wall.

I glared at him.

"Why?" I asked. "Too many witnesses here?"

"Just do it!" he growled, finally making eye contact. But when he saw me staring right back at him, he quickly looked away.

"You think because I'm small I'll take orders from you?" I fired back. "Guess again! In case you hadn't noticed, I'm not scared of you! And you can tell your friend Jacko that he doesn't scare me either!"

"Well then you're just crazy," he said. "Jacko will pulverize you."

"I've faced lots worse than Jacko McNulty, I can tell you that!" I barked. "I'm not afraid. You can give me your worst, but you can *never* make me back down!"

Dunk studied me curiously, like he was making his mind up about something important.

"So it's true then?" he asked.

"What are you talking about?" I nearly shouted.

But he didn't answer with words. Instead, he reached into his pocket and pulled out a small card. He hesitated a second, and then handed it to me. I lifted it up and read:

My eyes bugged out.

"No way," I gasped, staring up at him. "You, Duncan Williams, the big, tough, jock? You have a...?"

"Shut up!" he shouted angrily.

I still couldn't believe it.

"*You* want *my* help?"

He looked away again and fidgeted.

"Look, let's just not talk about this now," he said, but it sounded almost like he was pleading now. "Just meet me after school."

Then he finally looked back at me. Most of his face was as chiseled and smooth as a bowling ball, but his eyes were sunken and haunted in a way that I hadn't noticed before.

"OK," I agreed. "But not outside the locker room. Meet me in the library."

Dunk's face turned sour.

"The *library*?" he spat like it was a curse.

"That place where they store all the books. You *do* know where that is, don't you?" I scoffed. Dunk bit his lip.

"Why there?" he asked. "There'll be people all around..."

"People won't bother us there, and we can avoid your buddies, seeing as how I don't think they even know how to read. And I don't think you want them to see you hanging out with me discussing your...*problem*, do you?"

"N-no," he sputtered. "OK, the library. 3:00."

"I'll be there," I said.

Chapter Seven - Requirements

At the end of the school day I rushed out to the crosswalk where everyone was lining up for their buses and waited there to catch Jeannine before she climbed aboard the one that takes us home. I had already packed up my stuff and stopped in the office to call my mom and tell her that I was staying late, so I stood there tapping my foot, wondering if she was coming, or whether her mother had picked her up early to take her to rehearsal for that movie of hers. The big wall clock in the main office, which was visible through the huge glass windows that lined the front of the building, read 2:55, and I began worrying that I might end up being late for my meeting with Dunk at the library. I spun and scanned the scene one last time, thinking to myself that Jeannine would be much easier to spot if she still had those brightly colored streaks in her hair. But just as I gave up and turned to head off, my eyes caught sight of a mane of shimmery chocolate brown hair that was heading for bus #17. I knew it was her because of the way her head tilted back as she walked, like she was sniffing the air.

"Jeannine!" I called out breathlessly as I raced over to her. "It's a good thing I spotted you! I have to…"

"Oh Will, guess what?" she giggled gleefully as though she didn't hear me. "Remember Tiffany Jenkins? That nasty, spoiled brat who was teasing us before? Well, in English class today Timmy walked right up to her and said…"

"Um…Jeannine, I can't talk now. I'm taking the late bus today. Something came up. Something important."

Jeannine blinked like some bug had just flow into her eye.

"Really? And what could be so important?"

I took a deep breath, and my eyes shifted back and forth to make sure no one was watching, then I reached into my pocket for the magic business card, the one Dunk had given me, and showed it to her. At first Jeannine gasped, but then she looked up at me and smiled.

"Well, I guess you're back in business! Who's your new client?"

"I'll tell you all about it tomorrow. But do you have my MonsterScope? I need it back."

Jeannine frowned, but she reached into her backpack and pulled out what appeared to be a rather ordinary spyglass. Except there was nothing ordinary about it. When I took it from her hand, it throbbed, and grew warm in my fingers. The lens glowed with life, and through it everything seemed clearer, as though the world could hold no secrets.

"Thanks! Good thing you had it with you. You know I can't track down the monsters without it."

But Jeannine was still glaring at me.

"Will, you're not keeping me in suspense just to get even with me for not telling you earlier…?"

"No, nothing like that!" I cut in, quickly putting the scope away in my pocket. "It's just that…well, it's complicated. And I don't have time to explain now. I'm supposed to meet Dunk- er, my new client at the library. I'll call you later to…"

"Dunk? You can't mean Duncan Williams, the football star? You couldn't be helping *him*?"

I thought about that for a second.

"I…I couldn't be, could I?"

"Is it true? Is he your…"

Just then, our favorite bus driver bellowed, "Everybody on! NOW! Door closing!"

Jeannine quickly rushed off.

"You will tell me *everything*," she shouted back just before she climbed onto the bus.

Now, our school library is at the end of an isolated wing down in the oldest part of the school. My trek to get there from the bus stop took me down one hallway after another, each seemingly longer and darker than the last, and with each leg of the trip time seemed to roll backward. First I dashed down a bright, modern hallway lined with sparkling glass walls that welcomed in the sun, and next scampered through a hallway of pale green cinder block walls lit by long rows of stark florescent lights hanging down from steel suspension rods. By the time I got to the last hallway, whose antique brick and stone walls were lit by dim, dingy bulbs set high into the arched ceiling, my lungs felt like they would burst. Still, I made it to the library with time to spare. Thirty seconds to be exact. I would have smiled proudly, but I was doubled over, panting for air.

As it turned out, I needn't have worried.

When my breath returned, I straightened up and searched for my new client. Now you might think that he would be as easy to spot as a fox in a henhouse, being the most out of place person in the room, but it wasn't that simple. You see, our library is like one of those places that time forgot. It's a cramped, dark, and musty room lined with mahogany shelves from its concrete floor to the high, sculpted ceiling. Every corner is stacked with piles of books that have been sitting there since one of those old bald guys was president. The problem isn't that it's very big, it's just that with row after row of high book shelves crisscrossing the entire length of the room, you can't really see who is in there unless they are standing in the main aisle or right behind the counter at the far-side wall. And Dunk was nowhere to be seen. At first, I thought maybe he had changed his mind and decided not to show up, but as I walked down the aisle, a voice jumped out at me from behind one of the bookshelves.

"Over here," whispered a deep, brooding voice, I stepped around the shelf, and found Dunk leaning against it, his back to the wall, sitting on one of the stacked piles of old books. I stepped into the alcove and took a seat facing him on another pile. We stared at each other wordlessly, but then he looked down and began rubbing his knuckles. The silence held until Dunk finally glanced up and half-whispered, "So, you're a monster hunter, huh?"

"Monster *detective*," I corrected, and then pulled the Monster Detective Business Card from my pocket and handed it back to him. "Like it says on the card, see?"

"Uh, right," Dunk mumbled. He didn't say any more.

"So, how did you get that card, anyway?" I asked. Dunk's eyes sank like a rowboat made of tissue paper (something I actually built once – not one of my better experiments).

"I...I don't really know," he whispered. "Suddenly, it was just *there*."

"Just where?" But Dunk didn't answer. Instead, he began scratching his head and arms.

"Is this all for real?" He still seemed to have trouble getting any words out. "I mean, do you really...you know...?"

"Fight monsters?' I said softly, leaning in to be certain that no one else would hear. "Of course I do! Why else would I be here?"

"I don't know. It's just that you're, uh..." his eyes swung up at me, but then darted. "You're different than I expected. I though a monster detective would be, you know..."

"...Big and muscular with a face that looks like granite?" I finished for him.

"Well, yeah." He finally met my gaze. "You don't look like you could...you know..."

"...Win a fight against a butterfly, much less a monster?"

"Well, yeah."

I sat back and smiled, which just seemed to confuse Dunk.

"That's what all my clients think at first," I said. "But they all sing a different tune in the end. I've never yet met a monster I couldn't send crying home to its momma."

OK, that was stretching the truth a bit, seeing as how I'd only had one client so far, and one of his monsters might have swallowed me whole if Jeannine hadn't been there.

I exaggerated, OK? Infomercials do it all the time.

"'Really?" Dunk's eyes lit up. "Wow! Do you have some kind of...of super powers or something?"

I hesitated. Honestly, I liked the idea of having Duncan Williams, the big, hulking football player, think I might have super powers. It would definitely make him think twice before he picked on me ever again.

"Um, *something* like that."

"That is so cool! So, what's your power? Super strength? Super speed? Maybe we could use you on the football team!"

"I...I'm not a show off!" I growled. "It's not something I can do in public."

"But what is it?" he insisted. "What can you do?"

I glared at him, angry that he kept pressing the point, but then it occurred to me that if I was going to take his case he would eventually find out anyway, so I decided I might as well tell him.

"Look, I don't have eyes that shoot lasers or anything," I explained. "I just have a gift for tracking down monsters. That, plus some special tools for getting rid of them. I'm kind of like an exterminator, only without the van with a cockroach on top."

"What? That's it? You don't have special powers?"

"I do," I insisted. "I have special monster detection powers."

"What good is that? I don't need someone with monster detection powers! I already know where the monster is. What I need is someone with monster butt-kicking powers!"

"You know where the monster is?"

"Well, yeah! It's not like it's hiding, is it? It comes right on out and...and..." Dunk stuttered, and seemed to lose his nerve.

"Look," I said in a softer, more professional tone, "why don't we start from the beginning. Tell me about your..." I looked around again just to be sure no one was listening in. "...your *problem*."

"My problem? My problem is that I have a monster in my room, you idiot!"

My eyes narrowed, and my cheeks began to flare.

"Ye*sss*," I hissed through gritted teeth. "But you're going to have to give me a little more than that if you want my help.

Can you tell me a little bit about your monster? What it does? What it says?"

"What difference does it make?" Dunk growled. "You're a monster hunter, aren't you? You come, you find it, and you kick it's..."

"It doesn't work like that," I explained. "I need to know more about the monster to do my job."

Dunk fidgeted nervously.

"Like what?" he asked.

"Well, to get right down to it, I need to know..."

"Yeah?"

"...I need to know how it scares you."

Dunk jerked back. His face soured, but his eyes grew wide and his scratching turned fierce.

"Scares me?" he spat. "It doesn't scare me! Nothing scares me!"

"That's not true."

"Oh yeah? What makes you so sure, runt?"

"Simple," I said flatly. "You have a monster. Monsters are born when our fears grow so powerful that they take on a life of their own. No fears, no monster – that's how it works. So something scares you. Scares you real bad."

Dunk scowled. His face twitched and twisted like he had just forced down one of my mother's teriyaki tartlettes. Finally, he spewed out, "Didn't you see last week's game? When those two huge defensive linemen came down on me, I held my ground and got the ball to the receiver for a touchdown, even though I got pounded into the turf. That's what I do: Even if I get my head handed to me, I'm the one who gets it done. Does that sound like someone who gets scared?"

"No it doesn't," I admitted. Dunk nodded vigorously and stretched back into a self-satisfied grin, then added, "Darn right it doesn't!"

"But not being afraid of getting pounded by a couple of

goons," I countered, "isn't the same as not being afraid of *anything*. *I* should know. And if you ever want to be rid of your monsters, we need to find what you're afraid of so that you can overcome your fear of it. That's the only way you can conquer your monsters."

"What? Wait...you want *me* to fight the monsters? That's supposed to be *your* job."

"No it's not!"

"I thought you said you were a monster fighter!"

"Monster *Detective*, Mister Lard-for-brains! Like it says on the card! It's my job to help you see the truth about your monster so that you can face it, because monsters hide, and try to trick you with decoys, and disguise themselves. I help you see its true face."

"You don't know what you're talking about! My monster doesn't hide! It comes right out into the open for you to see!"

I was getting really riled at Dunk, but his last words surprised me, and made me forget all that.

"You see it?" I sputtered. "You actually know what it looks like?"

Dunk seemed taken aback.

"Yeah, I *see* it," he hissed. "Why, does that mean something bad?"

"Uh, no, not really," I replied. "It's just...unusual."

I didn't tell Dunk that I myself had never actually seen my own monster until Bigelow helped me. Neither had my other client, Timmy Newsome. The truth was, though, that I didn't know what that might mean, or even if it was important – a fact I had no intention of sharing with my new hotshot client.

"Well that gives us someplace to start then," I said. "Tell me *exactly* what you see."

Dunk's gaze locked on me for a moment, but then he looked away and shut his eyes.

"He comes from out of the shadows," Dunk whispered, keeping his eyes shut as he spoke. "He comes from...from *nothing*. And then he's there, right in front of me. This horrible figure in a dark, slimy robe."

"When does he appear?" I asked, though I pretty much knew the answer. "And where exactly are you when this happens?"

"It's always late at night, when I'm alone in my room," Dunk answered. "At first, the monster used to come right before I fell asleep. The first few times he appeared I was in bed, and I thought the whole thing was just a bad dream. But the last time he showed up it was earlier, when I was sitting at my desk thinking."

"You *think*?"

OK, maybe that was a cheap shot. Dunk glared at me, and I sort of corrected myself.

"Um, I mean *what* were you thinking about when the monster appeared?"

Dunk continued glaring, but then he looked away and went on with his story.

"I wasn't thinking about anything special. I was just sitting there and then I looked up and there he was. It was dark, real dark, because I had just put out my desk lamp and I couldn't see really well, but somehow he just... just appeared right in front of me. I squinted and blinked, thinking my eyes were playing tricks on me, but he was really there. His robe and hood covered him completely: face, hands, feet, everything. He just stood there and raised his hand. And his hand came out from the sleeve..."

Dunk shivered before continuing, "That hand was all withered and scabbed and slimy, and it had huge claws like a wild animal. And he pointed at me, and made this horrible moaning sound, and...and..."

"Yeah?"

"Well, It...it caught me by surprise, and I kind of...well, I fell out of my chair, but my foot landed on the desk and hit the switch on my desk lamp. The light came on, and when I got back up, the monster was gone."

"Did the monster speak to you, Dunk?"

"No, he…he doesn't say anything."

I can't say why, but I was certain that he was lying about that. For a moment, we just sat staring at each other, but I counted it as a sign that I was on the right track when Dunk broke eye contact first.

"Look, if you want my help, you've got to tell me the truth!"

"I told you, he doesn't speak!" he shouted. He looked up at me angrily, but then turned away again, and went silent.

"Fine," I finally growled, allowing Dunk a pass on that. "He doesn't say anything. But there *is* more. There has to be."

"What? I've told you everything!"

"There's more," I insisted. "Your monster is there for a reason. We need to know what that reason is."

"Well, I don't know what else to tell you! I don't know any more!"

"And that," I said smugly, "is why you need a monster detective."

Chapter Eight – Transmission Problems

All the way home on the late bus that afternoon, I sat thinking about my puzzling new case. So many things made no sense – like why would Dunk lie about the monster? I was certain he hadn't been telling the truth about the monster not speaking, just as I knew without a doubt that I needed to find out what it said in order to solve the case. But why would Dunk lie to me when he needed my help?

Then again, the real mystery was: why was I helping him at all? Duncan Williams was a liar, a bully, and who knows what else. He was a bad person. Why shouldn't I just leave him to his monster and be done with it?

I was still lost in thought when I stepped in through the door of my house to find my mother right in front of me, telephone in hand.

"Will!" she said with same exasperation in her voice that she had when she found me trying to sew a MP3 player into the sleeve of my jacket. "This phone call is for you! Would you take it please? It's Jeannine, and this is already her fourth call this afternoon trying to reach you!"

"I thought I lost my phone privileges?"

"You've got them back. Your punishment is over. Now just take the phone, please?"

I grimaced.

"Couldn't you keep punishing me for just a few minutes more?"

"I HEARD THAT!" Jeannine's voice roared from the receiver.

My mother smirked at me with one of those bemused *'You're in for it now'* kind of looks. I sighed.

"Oh, all right," I groaned as she handed me the phone. I bit my lip, and then bellowed in an artificially cheery voice, "Hi Jeannine! What's up?"

"I'm in the car on the way to rehearsal," she said. "But I borrowed my mom's cell phone because I just couldn't wait. You've got to tell me: is it true? Is your new client really Duncan Williams?"

I smiled, and actually considered keeping her in suspense for a while, but in the end I decided it wasn't worth the grief she would give me for it.

My dad calls stuff like that 'interpersonal diplomacy'. He always uses fancy words when he does whatever my mom wants him to do.

"It's true," I answered. Jeannine let out a weird sound, half gleeful laugh, half gasp.

Hey, if you don't think that's a weird sound, *you* try doing it.

"I can't believe it!" She chortled. "I can't believe it! This is such poetic justice!"

"What's poetry got to do with it?"

"It's an expression," she said with her familiar, haughty tone jumping out of the receiver at me. "One you would know if you..."

"All right, never mind," I interrupted. "Yes, he is my client, and yes, I'm going to his house tonight. If I can find a way to get there, that is."

"Get where?"

"I've got the address right here: 3212 Hester Street, wherever that is."

"Hester Street? Isn't that down by the old K-Mart?"

"Is it? Oh man, that's, like, 30 blocks! It'll take me an hour to walk there!"

"Well, you could get there faster if you run."

"Jeannine, I'm a monster detective, not a track star."

"Hmmm," she hummed as she thought. "Don't you have a bicycle?"

"Not one that works. My old cycle is too small for me."

"Well then," Jeannine chimed. "Isn't it time you got a new one?"

"Sure," I replied. "But try telling that to my parents."

"Come on, Will," Jeannine droned impatiently. "Just tell them that you need a new bicycle. How hard could it be?"

"Are you kidding? Haven't you ever met my parents?"

"Oh, Will," she chided. "For a courageous monster detective, sometimes you can be such a wuss."

Well, *that* was an annoying conversation. It's not like I expected any better: Jeannine is a good and loyal friend, but she has never been the gentle, sympathetic type. Still, it was a low blow for her to question my bravery, what with all we've been through together. I mean, I love my mom and dad, but Jeannine just doesn't understand what an absolute horror it is to try and talk to them about stuff like this. And yes, I'm a fearless monster detective and all that, but if I have a choice between facing some slimy, green creature with razor-sharp fangs ready to eat me alive, or trying to convince my dad that I need a new bicycle…well, let's just say that it's much more likely that the horrible monster will give me a big slobbery kiss than it is that my dad will cough up a single dime.

Still. I had to try, right?

"If you want it that badly," my dad said from behind the sports section of the newspaper that he held up between us as he sat in his lounge chair, "get a job and earn the money for it yourself. Mow some lawns, or walk some dogs. You can't really appreciate something unless you work hard and earn it."

"I *do* work hard," I said. "Every term I get straight 'A's, even though…"

"I meant at a job," my father interrupted.

I glared at him. I debated with myself whether to say what was on my mind, but in the end, there was no holding back.

"I *have* a job," I stated firmly. My dad lowered his paper just enough to meet my stare over the top of the page.

"Fine," he finally said, raising the paper back up again. "Then use the money you earn from your…*job*…to buy yourself the bike you want."

"It doesn't work that way," I grumbled. "My clients are kids. They don't have the money to pay me enough for a bicycle."

"Then maybe you should find new clients," my dad said. "Or a better paying job."

I frowned. I knew my dad didn't take my job seriously. Neither of my parents really believes that I fight monsters, but then no grownup would, seeing as how adults can't even see them.

"Fine," I finally agreed. "But to do that I'll need reliable transportation. If you want me to get a job, I need the bicycle first."

I smiled slyly, thinking that I had outfoxed my dad with an argument he himself had set me up for. I was convinced that I had talked myself into at least a sturdy three-speed with an electric horn and high-beam headlight, but then my dad spoke up again, and squashed that idea like a bug on a windshield.

"You won't even use it for more than a few weeks," he said. "Pretty soon you won't want to be seen on a bike anymore. Then you'll be coming back to me asking for a new car instead."

"Dad, I'm not even twelve yet! It'll be years before I can drive, much less own a car!"

Faced with irrefutable logic, there was only one thing my father could say.

"Go ask your mother," he grumbled as he ruffled his paper and turned the page.

I just stared at him. Choosing between continuing to plead with the back of my dad's newspaper or talking to the back of my mother's paint splattered canvas was like deciding whether to walk barefoot through a pig sty or spit into the wind.

But I had to try, right?

I found my mom down in her painting studio in the basement, furiously dabbing away with her brush at some poor, defenseless canvas. I casually stepped around behind her to look at what she was doing, and my eyes were attacked by glaring blotches of scarlet, ginger, and mahogany splattered all over the surface.

"I...I like it," I said. "It's...nice."

"It's nice?" she said skeptically. "Really? What exactly is

nice about it?"

"I, um...I like the mix of colors. It's really bright and cheery. What do you call it?"

"A Season of Sorrows."

I winced. My mom wiped her brow, and then began squeezing more paint onto her palette.

"So," she said casually without looking back at me, "What is it you want?"

"What makes you think I want something?"

This time my mother *did* turn around. She glared at me and said, "You wanted something, but your father wouldn't go for it, so you came down here to talk me into it instead. Now what was it?"

"How...how did you know that?" I spluttered. My mom just rolled her eyes at me.

"Oh, let's see," she muttered. "First there was the guitar. Then the new baseball bat. Then the camera. So what is it this time?"

I just stared at her. You know, my mother might make a pretty good detective herself. If she wasn't a grown-up.

"A bicycle," I confessed. My mom nodded, and turned back to her canvas with a smug grin spreading across her face.

"Don't you already have a bicycle?"

"Well, sort of..."

"Sort of?"

"I need a *new* bike," I pleaded. "My old one is just too small."

"Don't be silly," my mom said. "You can still get another good year or two out of it."

"I can't," I maintained. "The seat is already almost as high as it can go."

"Almost doesn't count," she said. "Just raise it some more."

"But when I raise the seat higher my knees bang against

the handlebars when I pedal."

My mother turned and stared hard at me up and down, but then turned back to her painting.

"I'm sure you can manage."

As she spoke, she dabbed her paintbrush in a blob of aqua blue paint on her palette, and then smeared it into a big glob of fire engine red and began mixing.

"Come on, Mom!" I argued, "I can't go riding around the neighborhood in a bike that's too small for me. I might as well be on a tricycle!"

"Well, we still have one in the garage if you..."

"Mom, just tell me why! Why can't I have a new bicycle?"

"Because money is tight right now, and it's just not something you need," she said flatly.

"I *do* need it," I argued. "This is important!"

"No, you just *think* it's important," she insisted.

"I think I can decide for myself what's important to me!" I growled as my cheeks turned nearly the same shade of purple as the paint on her brush. My mom just shrugged me off.

"Of course you say that," she said dismissively. "But you'll think differently when you're older." And then she splattered her canvas with more random dots of paint.

"Come on, Mom," I pleaded. "I need to go all the way across town! If I can't get a bike, then at least can I get a ride over to Dunk's house?"

"Is this for more of your Monster..."

"No!" I growled angrily. I didn't want to lie, but really, what choice did I have? "I'm...I'm his math tutor."

My mother glared at me suspiciously, but then finally mumbled, "Fine." She turned toward the stairwell and called out, "James! A moment of your precious time, please!"

Well, you can bet that my mom doesn't call out for my dad very often, because he came running like the house was on fire. He burst through the door and bounded down the steps two at a time, but...

OK, I should explain that the reason that my mom's studio is in the basement is because it's the only thing the space down there is good for, seeing as how the ceiling is only around five and a half feet high. In his hurry to reach us, my dad must have forgotten that little fact, which is a really bad thing for someone who is nearly six feet tall to do.

A seventy-one inch tall man rushing into a sixty-eight inch high room – do the math. As he reached the bottom of the stairs, my dad banged the top of his head dead-on into a low-hanging beam. He flipped over like a cartoon character and landed on his back.

"Owww!" He moaned, as he grabbed his head with his hand.

"James! Are you all right?" my mother asked.

My dad said nothing. He just sat himself up and grasped the railing, one hand still gingerly holding his head like it was a dented pumpkin. He pulled himself up, and then marched unsteadily back up the stairs and out of sight. When he returned, he was holding a bag of frozen peas to his head. He stepped carefully back down the stairs, and glared at the beams in the ceiling like it was their fault he banged his head on them. The bag of peas slipped for a moment, and you could see the huge lump underneath. My mother seemed mesmerized by it, and she moved in for a closer look. She examined the swelling bruise carefully, and prodded it with her finger.

"Owww!" My dad moaned, and my mom instantly pulled her finger away.

"Sorry. Does it hurt?" she asked.

"No, I'm wearing this bag of frozen peas on my head as a fashion statement!" he howled. "Which reminds me – why don't we have an ice pack in the freezer? They're pretty handy to have around, you know!"

My mom just nodded, though it was hard to hide the

smirk on her face.

"Now what was so important that I had to come rushing down here?" my father demanded

"Yes, Will, what was so important?" my mom said slyly.

I glared at my mother as my father's gaze turned and burned down at me. Finally, I turned to my dad, cleared my throat, and said quietly, "I, um…I need a ride."

My dad looked at me like I was speaking Chinese.

"A what?" he mumbled.

"A ride, dad! A ride!" I hissed impatiently. "You know, where we get in the car, and the wheels turn round and round, and we go places?"

"Don't you take that tone with me, young man! If you think we're going to take you wherever you want to go whenever you feel like it…"

"Well I wouldn't need for you to take me places," I growled, "if you would get me a new bicycle!"

"Oh, let's not get started on that again," my mom grumbled. "And by the way, Will, if you want people to help you when you need it, perhaps you should try being a little more helpful yourself? Like by raking the yard without having to be asked ten times, or remembering to hang up your clothes?"

Isn't it just like a mom to try and turn things around on you like that? Meanwhile, my dad was already losing interest in the whole thing. He took the bag of peas off his forehead, and muttered, "Enough."

Right then, I had to hold back a sudden fit of giggles – you see, the ink from the bag had left an imprint on my dad's head. His left temple now looked like it had a big purple and green tattoo of a plate of peas on it. I looked at my mom, who chuckled, but covered her mouth to hold in her laughing. My dad just gave us a puzzled look.

"What?" he grumbled? "What's so funny?"

My mom just bit her lip and squeezed out the words, "Oh,

nothing…nothing at all," between the tight fingers across her mouth.

My dad glared at us suspiciously, but then turned and walked back up the stairs, grumbling something under his breath. My mother grinned.

"Third time he's done that this month," she giggled to herself. "This just never gets old."

Needless to say, I made my own way to Dunk's house.

Chapter Nine – Saber Rattling

I don't know which was worse: the gash I got in my hand when the wrench slipped as I was adjusting my bicycle seat, the bruises I got on my knees from banging them into the handlebars as I pedaled, or the snickers of the people I passed as I squeaked by on a bike so small that riding it made me look like a graduate from clown college. On top of all that, at the intersection of Jefferson and LaMonte Avenues my rear wheel got stuck in a sewer grating and I almost got run over while trying to yank it out. Then I got scrapes on my hands, a bruise on my elbow, and a gash in my pants when my coat got tangled in the gears and pitched me forward over the handlebars.

"This thing is going to kill me," I grumbled as I righted myself, and then walked my bike the rest of the way. When I finally got to Dunk's house, I propped it up against the mailbox, owing to the lack of a kickstand, and left it there as I stepped up to the door.

OK, maybe I kicked the stupid thing once, but then I focused on the job ahead of me. I looked up at the door, which was several crumbling concrete steps up from the street, bordered by rusty iron railings that were a bit lopsided. Above the threshold, a silhouette of wispy purple clouds clawed across the rickety roof. The door itself was old, engraved, and heavy-looking, with a mosaic of stained glass embedded into the dark oak frame. It was definitely the fanciest looking door among the series of row houses that lined the block, but also the most weathered. I stepped up and reached for the doorbell, but the button was missing, and loose wires were hanging from the wall in its place. Instead, I opened the frayed screen door and knocked. When there was no answer, I knocked again, more loudly.

"Hold yo' horses, I'm a-comin'!" called out a loud, deep voice from within. I could hear a sloppy, shuffling sound approach the door just before there was some rumbling and clicking, and then a heavy groan followed as the door yawned open. My feet involuntarily slid back, because there in the space where the door had been was something even bigger and heavier blocking the entry.

"Um...Is this Duncan Williams' house?" I inquired meekly.

"Yah," the huge man mumbled, motioning with his hand for me to enter. "Come on, come on..." Then he turned and began walking away without looking back. I tried looking up at the man as I followed his long, uneven strides into the house, but he was so big and the hallway so dark and narrow that I couldn't see past his huge, broad back and shoulders, which were covered by a faded blue flannel robe filled with pictures of Popeye the sailor Now, you might think that a man covered with cartoon characters from head to foot looked pretty silly, but this guy was big enough that no one was ever going to tell him so. With nothing else to look at but the walls, I couldn't help noticing that they were covered in grainy wood paneling the color of my mother's jeans. Now, I'm no decorator or anything, but really - what were they thinking?

"Are you Dunk's father?" I asked meekly.

"Yah, yah. Come on in da livin' rum. He'll be down in a sec," he answered.

"DUNCAN! SOMEBODY HERE FOR YOU, RIGHT?" the man suddenly bellowed so loud that his voice hit me in the head like a sledgehammer.

"CHILL OUT, I'M COMING ALREADY!" Dunk's voice echoed back.

Dunk came bounding down the stairs two at a time, and jumped to the floor from the fifth step. He seemed quite pleased with his landing, but then looked up and saw me, and the color drained from his face.

"Oh...uh, hi Will," he mumbled. His face and posture slumped as if his dentist had just made a house call, but then his eyes caught his father's curious stare, and he instantly straightened.

It's funny, but seeing him standing there side by side with his father gave me a whole different view of Duncan Williams. At school Dunk was an imposing figure, standing tall and broad as he swaggered around among his classmates, but his father must have been a head taller and a foot wider, with skin that was a much darker shade of brown than his son. He towered over Dunk pretty much the same way Dunk towers over the rest of us. But though the man's broad shoulders were swollen with huge, heavy muscles, his waistline bulged even more, and had fought its way loose from under the ratty old Chicago Bears t-shirt he wore under his robe. It was clear that he had grown a lot in that area in the since he had bought the clothes he wore.

"So, boyo...Who's yo' lil' friend?" his father asked.

"This is Will Allen," Dunk said uncomfortably. "He's our new...uh, mascot..."

"Math Tutor," I injected too late. "I'm Dunk's new Math tutor."

Dunk's dad gave me a suspicious look, like he thought I was lying (which, of course, I *was*). He squinted as though he was trying to figure out what we might be really up to, but I guess all that thinking burned out his brain cells, because he finally just sighed and clapped Dunk on the back. Hard.

"Good," he said. "Dem scouts, dey like a player who work hard at his studies. Way to plan ahead, boyo."

Then he turned, shuffled with a slight limp back into the living room, and slumped loudly into an easy chair. Dunk watched him there with a strange look on his face. As I looked at him, an odd sensation came over me, as though the feelings behind that expression were reaching out to me, but before I could reflect much on that Dunk suddenly turned and grabbed me by the shoulder and began pushing me toward the stairs.

"Come on," he hissed quietly. "Let's go."

When we got to Dunk's room, he quickly forced us inside and shut the door. Then he turned back to me and shoved me with both hands.

"What do you think you're doing?" he shouted. "Are you trying to get me in trouble, you little..."

"Keep your hands off me!" I shouted, shoving him right back. For a moment, Dunk's eyes narrowed, and I thought we might come to blows. Instead, he straightened himself, but then yelled, "Why did you say you're a...a tutor?" He spat the word like it was a curse.

"Well, *excuse* me," I hissed back. "But if you don't want your dad to know why I'm really here, maybe you should let me know what lie to tell him *before* he asks!"

At first Dunk's eyes remained fierce, but then he blinked, and shook his head a bit.

"Right," he grumbled. "OK, right. Let's just get on with it then."

Dunk turned away, like he'd already forgotten about the whole thing, but my eyes were still burning. Dunk walked over to his desk and announced, "This is the spot. This is where he appeared last time."

I just stood there, still fuming, but then grabbed my MonsterScope from my pocket and walked to the desk.

"What's that?" Dunk asked.

"My MonsterScope," I answered. "It reveals traces of the

monsters - where they've been and what they've touched. That way we can figure out what they're after." And without another word, I began examining the desk.

Now, I've only used my MonsterScope a couple of times, but it's pretty simple how it works: when you look through it, normal stuff looks like it always does, but monster stuff glows.

Well, I *thought* that was how it works, but when I looked through it this time, I couldn't see *anything*. I tried to peer through the glass, but it was all smoky.

"Just a sec," I mumbled. "The lens must be dirty."

But no matter how much I wiped it, the lens remained filled with fog, and impossible to see through.

"What's going on?" I grumbled to myself, and shook the scope like a rattle.

Yes, I know that never helps. I don't know why everybody does that when things don't work. It's one of the great mysteries of life.

""Problem?" Dunk asked.

I glared at him. The last thing I wanted to do at this point was admit to jerk-boy that I didn't have things under control.

So I faked it.

"No problem," I replied, then turned and began examining the room, looking at everything through my foggy, useless MonsterScope. I walked all around, taking in everything from the 'I'm a spoiled brat' flat screen TV to the rows of 'I'm a smug, coddled athlete' trophies. Dunk's desk was like my dad's: big, heavy, and mahogany, topped with a messy clutter of books, papers, mugs filled with pens, a laptop computer, and lots of bits of junk. I might almost have been fooled into thinking that he was a hard-working student if I didn't already know he was a brainless jock. His room didn't have a lot of other furniture, just the desk, a matching end table, and a chest of drawers, but unlike the rest of the house everything was neat, clean, and tidy. Except for the mess on the desk, it looked just like a furniture store showroom, from the TV on the wall to the perfectly made bed with a football-shaped headboard, which was covered in a Chicago Bears Bedspread that matched his blue and red striped wallpaper.

"Wow," I muttered, looking up and checking out Dunk's walls, which were filled with sports pictures, banners, and memorabilia-filled shadow boxes. One in particular caught my eye.

"Is that really…"

"Heyman Randolph's jersey," Dunk finished for me. "Yeah, he gave it to me himself."

"You met him?"

"My dad played with him. I've met him loads of times."

I whistled, and then continued across the wall, looking at all of the cool stuff hanging on it. There were lots more photos: some were of Dunk holding up trophies, while others were action shots of people playing football. One particularly old and worn frame contained a photo of Dunk's dad shaking hands with some guy in a suit while being handed a plaque which read, "Sportsman of the Year, 1979". Another had a photo of Dunk surrounded by a bunch of cheerleaders, who were gazing admiringly at him like he was some kind of hero. A few feet further down was a long shelf covered with an endless string of trophies, and just past the end of it was another framed picture, different than the others in that it was smaller and encased in a plain black frame. Still, though it was inexpensively framed, it was much cleaner and better cared for than the others. In the picture, Dunk was held aloft on the shoulders of his teammates, including Truck, Jacko, and several of the goons from the bathroom.

"This year's team?" I asked.

"Last year's," Dunk replied. "Most of us were just 7th graders then, but we won the conference championship." His eyes, swollen with insufferable pride, shifted from me to the photo, and began to grow misty. "I threw the winning touchdown pass with 6 seconds left. A 32 yarder to Jacko. He told me later that I threw it so hard it almost knocked him over. Of course..." He looked back at me. "...I didn't actually see the catch. A defensive lineman speared me in the back the moment I released the ball."

"Wow. That must have really hurt."

"Nah. When you play football, taking hits is part of the game. You can't let pain or anything else get to you. You put it aside and focus on what you came to do."

"Funny. It's the same doing what I do."

"Fighting monsters?"

"No, *bullies*."

Dunk's eyes suddenly turned fierce.

"I am not a bully!" He shouted.

"Oh really?" I shot back. "Well what do you call it when a bunch of big strong football players get together to pick on one tiny little kid?"

"Look, it's your own fault for messing with my guys."

"It was them who messed with me! You were there. You saw what they did – what *you* did! You picked on Gerald for no reason!"

"Oh, stop your whining! Nobody wants to hear it."

"You think it's OK? You think its OK to pick on people just because you're bigger and stronger than them?"

"Well, wake up, Junior! That's how the world is. I didn't make it that way. I'm just living in it, the same as you."

"You are not the same as me! You're *nothing* like me! You're the one who's supposed to be top dog and everything! If you weren't a bully, you would make your guys stop instead of helping them do it!"

Dunk cringed.

"Oh yeah? Well what would *you* do? What would you do if some punk who was way smaller than you was mouthing off? The same as them, the same as me, I'll bet!"

"I would not! I'd never take advantage of people smaller than me! I would never do mean things just because I could get away with it!"

"Oh, really? Then why did you call me Mister Lard-for-brains back at the library? That was pretty mean."

"I said it because you were acting so stupid!"

"You said it," Dunk insisted, "because you knew you would get away with it. We were in the library with people all around. I was looking for your help. You knew I wouldn't do anything to you."

"It's not the same! It's not the same as bullying someone!"

"Look, I'm just saying you should stop pretending that you're some kind of saint or something. If you were bigger and stronger, you'd take advantage just like anyone else."

"That is not true!"

My cheeks were hot and as red as a fire hydrant, and if my eyes really could shoot lasers, Dunk would have been toast. But at just that moment, a cold shudder raced across my shoulders, as though a hand of ice had suddenly gripped me. I turned and scanned all around looking for the source, but there was nothing in sight.

"There's something here," I whispered, dropping into a crouch and slowly turning my head back and forth.

"Re-really?" Dunk stuttered. "Are you sure?"

I nodded. "Turn out the light."

"What? Are you nuts?"

"You have to," I said, glaring up at him. "The monster won't come out when the light is on. If you want to get rid of this thing, we've got to lure him out."

Dunk's eyes nearly popped from their sockets and his fingers absent-mindedly clawed at his face, but he nodded, and did as I told him. The room went dark, but bits of light came in through the window from the night sky outside. Strangely though, the light pouring in died out in several spots across the floor, as though a shadow from out of nowhere had fallen upon them. From those shadows, a deep, inky blackness began to spread through the room. I instinctively pulled out my only weapon.

"What's that?" Dunk asked.

"It's my special flashlight, the RevealeR," I answered, flicking the switch. "It's what I use to fight the monsters."

"That's how you fight monsters? You must be yanking my chain! That stupid thing? It barely even lights up!"

I scowled, but Dunk was right – the beam from my RevealeR was really weak. Instead of light, something more like waves of smoke came pouring out. The shadows surrounding us closed in like floodwaters, and I swung the RevealeR all around the room, but the smoky beam was swallowed up by the darkness.

"It'll light up just fine," I assured him. "Just give it a minute. It'll light up and shrivel your monsters like a prune, as long as..."

"As long as what?" Dunk asked.

I didn't answer, because at that very moment, something suddenly emerged from the shadows: a large, flat, wavy silhouette that was somehow even darker than the blackness surrounding it. The...I don't know what to call it...*the shadow darker than shadows*, fluttered above us like a flag in the wind, and then began floating down. As it lowered, it began to drape what appeared to be an invisible human form, creating a cloak of darkness upon arms, head, body, and legs. The dark sheet kept falling until it covered the entire form like a burial shroud.

Then something within *moved*. The top of the thing - its *head* I would guess, leaned back, and a hollow moaning sound filled the room. Dunk froze, but his hand shot out and grabbed my arm so tight it cut off the blood to my fingers.

"Well come on!" he stuttered. "There he is! Shine that stupid flashlight of yours on it already!"

I pulled my arm out of his grasp and aimed my RevealeR right at the...whatever it was, but the smoky beam, if it did anything at all, actually made the figure even harder to see. The shadow-robed figure swelled larger, and the moaning grew louder.

"Ah, small problem there," I muttered as I shook the flashlight vigorously, willing it to light. "It's not working!"

"Not working! Are you kidding me?!"

"Yes, I'm really in a joking mood at the moment!" I growled.

"Well do something!"

"Without the RevealeR, I've got nothing!"

Dunk shook, and fumed, until finally he exploded.

"I knew it!" He shouted. "I knew you were just jerking me around! A little twerp like you fighting monsters? Who are you kidding?"

I didn't answer as the flood of darkness swirled around us, closing in tight about our legs like the tentacles of an octopus. They began pulling us in deeper, and I griped my RevealeR as tight as I could in hopes of squeezing something out of it. Dunk fought against the pull, but even as he backed away, there was a loud slashing sound.

"Yeeoow! It's attacking!" Dunk shouted, jerking and spinning on the spot. "Something just hacked at me! I think I'm bleeding!"

"Don't panic! The monster just wants to..." I called out, but at that very moment, there was another slashing sound, and the sleeve of my jacket was sliced wide open. I pointed my RevealeR into the darkness, but nothing was exposed. Powerless, as the swirls of darkness enveloped me I cried out, "Dunk! Find light switch! Quick, turn the light back on!"

"But you told me..."

"I know what I told you! Just hit the lights!"

Dunk fought his way back to the wall and then fumbled across it to the switch. He flicked it, and the room instantly filled with light. I squinted from the sudden brightness, and by the time I finished blinking, the shadows and the dark, blanketed figure were all gone as if they had never been there. I looked over at Dunk, who was panting heavily and holding his forearm.

"Are...are you...OK?"

"Just get out of here!" Dunk growled, throwing his head into his hands. "I must have been crazy, thinking someone like you could...imagining you were..." Then he glared up at me. "And if anyone at school hears one word of this I will personally..."

"Don't worry!" I hissed right back. "I don't want anyone to know about this any more than you do!" And then I stormed out of the room, down the stairs, and out the door to climb onto my man-eating bicycle for the ride home.

Chapter Ten – Heated Conversations

The ride home from Dunk's house was even more painful than the one going there, mainly because all of the scrapes and bruises I had gotten earlier had begun to swell and throb. I didn't realize how bad they looked though, not until...

"*Aiiieeee!*" my mother screamed as I slunk through the front door of our house and into the foyer.

"What happened to you?" she gasped as she staggered toward me and looked me over. "Did this happen to you when you were...?" She hesitated, and then spun to my father, who was sitting in his chair reading the newspaper. As if by instinct, he lowered the paper so that he could see over the top.

"You see?" my mom shouted at him. "I told you what would happen if we let him carry on with that crazy..."

"It was my bicycle!" I injected angrily. "All these cuts and bruises happened when I was fixing it, riding it, or getting ejected from it! None of this has anything to do with my...my *tutoring*."

My mother turned and eyed me suspiciously. She grabbed my hand and examined the gash on it.

"The wrench slipped when I was adjusting the seat," I explained. She mumbled, "Mmm hmm," and grabbed my other hand, yanking my shoulder painfully. I yelped.

"The scrapes are from when I fell off," I moaned.

"You cry out like that from a little scrape?"

"No," I growled. "From having my arm yanked from its socket!" And I pulled my hand out of her grasp. My mom glared down at me, but then turned again to my father, who simply shrugged, and then slipped back behind his newspaper. My mother bit her lip, slowly brought her hands together, and took a long, deep breath. Then she gazed back at me again.

"Those cuts and scrapes need to be cleaned and bandaged," she said firmly, and then turned and walked to the kitchen. She paused at the door.

"And don't think this is going to get you a new bicycle," she called back. "Contrary to popular opinion, I am *not* a sucker for a good sob story." Then she continued on into the kitchen. My dad rustled the newspaper, and went back to his reading.

You know, one of the best things about my parents is that they are really keen on teaching me to be independent by letting me take care of myself. Of course, that's also one of the *worst* things about them too, seeing as how they are usually nowhere to be found when I need help. Like when I was trying to clean and bandage my own hands, for example.

Hey, it's trickier than you think! Go ahead, try getting a bandage to stay in place on the palm of your hand when both hands are covered with slimy antiseptic cream, why don't you? It took me six bandages, fourteen pieces of sterile tape, and about a thousand cuss words before I got it to stick. Still, that wasn't the worst part. It wasn't the scolding from my mom, or my dad fading into his newspaper, or the burning pain from having to wash out my cuts and scrapes either. No, the worst part was that I was all beaten up, and neither the bully nor the monsters had anything to do with it.

"Not exactly the proud battle scars of a fearless hero," I muttered to myself as I sat at my desk looking over my scratched up hands. "Good thing Bigelow can't see me now."

"But I *can* see you," called out a scratchy, gravelly voice. My eyes instinctively sought out the source, and traced it to my bed, where my old Teddy Bear sat at the base of my pillow.

"Teddy!" I whispered. "You're back! But that must mean..."

"I'm back too," the voice echoed. And even as the sound of the voice faded, a lump began to form beneath my blanket right beside Teddy. It swelled and grew until it rose almost three feet above the top of the bed. The blanket rustled, and then flew into the air, revealing the form of my friend and mentor, Bigelow Hawkins, the great monster detective. His oversized trench coat and bowler hat hung loosely from his munchkin-sized form, and covered him so completely that the only visible part of him was some scraggly hair that stuck out from under the hat. He hopped down off the bed, smoothed the wrinkles in his coat (which only caused even bigger creases to form) and straightened his hat. I just gaped at him.

"Bigelow..." I muttered. "You're here!"

"I am indeed!" he replied. "Pleased to see me?"

There was an awkward silence as I remained frozen, torn between different impulses of what to say. Finally, one of them took hold.

"What happened to you?" I bellowed. "I had a new case, and I needed your help! Where were you?"

"Fishing," Bigelow answered calmly. "Like I wrote in my note. And let me tell you, Teddy and I caught one of the biggest..."

"How could you do that?" I cried out. "How could you go off fishing when I needed you? I thought you were supposed to help me!"

Bigelow recoiled.

"Are you saying that I should always be sitting around

waiting for the moment you call out for help?"

"I, um… well, no," I mumbled, suddenly less animated. "But don't you *know* when I need you?"

"Not before it happens. The future is inscrutable, Will."

"It's…what?"

"Inscrutable. Hard to read. Impossible to predict. But enough of this. I am here now. What can I help you with?"

"Well, I got a new case that's giving me trouble. Actually, it's not the *case* giving me trouble, so much as my new client, Duncan Williams. He's a big, bullying football player who likes to pick on little kids. The big jerk even tried to pick on *me*! Anyway, my problem is that I couldn't get my MonsterScope or RevealeR to work."

"No," Bigelow said flatly. "That is not your problem."

"It…it is!" I insisted. "My MonsterScope was all fogged up, and my RevealeR wouldn't light!"

"And do you know why your RevealeR would not light?" Bigelow asked.

"Of course I do!" I answered heatedly. "You taught me that the RevealeR is powered by understanding, so if there was no light, it was because I didn't understand Dunk's monster! But how could I? He didn't tell me anything!"

But Bigelow shook his head.

"Oh, but he did, Will," he said. "He told you a great deal. You are simply not ready to understand."

"Bigelow, how can you say that!" I sputtered. "You weren't there! You don't even *know* Duncan Williams!"

"No, I don't," Bigelow agreed. "I know *you*. And I sense that you have feelings that make it impossible for you to solve this case. Feelings that can paralyze even a brave monster detective."

"I'm not afraid!" I shouted. "I can handle anything Dunk's monsters dish out!"

Bigelow remained quiet, studying me as I spewed quick, fiery breaths. When he spoke, his voice was a soft, raspy rattle.

"I believe you, Will. But fear is not always the only feeling that you need to overcome. Conquering fear without controlling your other feelings can cause your RevealeR to behave...improperly."

"Behave improperly?" I sputtered. "How?"

"We shall see. Take out your RevealeR," Bigelow instructed.

I did as he told me.

"Now turn it on."

My thumb pushed down on the switch, but nothing happened.

"You see?" I grumbled.

"I do indeed," Bigelow said. "Now, think about Duncan Williams. Think about all the things that happened today, the things he did."

Images immediately sprung into my mind. Dunk's nasty leer in the lunchroom. His threats in the boy's room. The way he grabbed me and shoved me in his room. His insults. My free hand clenched tight into a fist, and my face flushed hot and red. The more I thought about Dunk, the more my blood boiled, but still the RevealeR would not light.

"So?" I growled. "Nothing has changed!"

"Are you sure? Look again at your RevealeR."

At first, I didn't understand what Bigelow was talking about, but then I held the RevealeR up and noticed that there *was* something flowing out of it. The same dark waves that had streamed out in Dunk's room were gushing once more. They spilled out into my room, darkening everything they touched. My desk and my bed grew hazy and difficult to see. I shook the casing in my hand vigorously, but the mud-like current continued pouring from its face.

"Yeah, but look!" I barked. "All that comes out is...is smoke!"

"That is what *you* see," Bigelow explained. "But this..."

he took out his own RevealeR and pointed its light at the beam flowing from mine. "This is what *I* see."

And then I screamed.

All around me, everything was burning. The light from Bigelow's RevealeR showed waves of fire flowing from my flashlight like a flamethrower. They engulfed everything they touched in a dark blaze like some low level of Hades.

"Yaaaaahh!" I screeched, shaking my RevealeR, struggling with the switch to try and turn it off. When that didn't work, I tried to drop it like a hot potato, but the RevealeR seemed to be glued to my hand, almost as though it was holding me as much as I was holding it. "Bigelow, what did you do!?"

"It is not what *I* have done," Bigelow said without the slightest bit of alarm. "I am simply revealing what *you* have done."

"Are you crazy?!" I shouted, still struggling as my desk ignited, along with everything on it. My drapes began to burn, and my bedposts turned into torches. My baseball glove, my computer, my books - *everything* caught fire, and I stood there helplessly as my entire room was engulfed in flames.

"Bigelow!" I shouted. "Help me! Make it stop!"

"I can't. *You* must make it stop, Will," he said.

"How?" I cried, trying not to panic. "I have no water! I have no fire extinguisher! I have *nothing!*"

"You're wrong, Will," Bigelow said, his voice as soft as his gravelly growl can sound. "You have a way to put out the flames. Master the fire within you."

"What? What are you talking about?"

"Control yourself, Will," Bigelow instructed calmly. "Master your feelings. Do that and you will conquer the flames."

"HOW?!" I screamed desperately.

"You will douse the flames when you are calm, and in control of your emotions."

"*Calm*?!" I screeched. "How can I be calm when everything is on fire?!"

"To calm yourself, you must focus on something that soothes you to quiet the rage." And then Bigelow reached behind his back and brought forward...

"My Teddy?" I snatched my Teddy Bear from Bigelow's grasp and cradled it like a mother wolf protecting her cubs. Strangely, that did soothe me a little. Teddy's soft fur seemed to radiate peace and comfort, and some of the tension in my body eased.

"Good," Bigelow said. "Now, close your eyes. Focus on taking control of your breathing, just as you do when facing monsters. Inhale deeply, and make your breaths slow and steady."

I shut my eyes and tried to breathe deeply like he said, but it was hard. At first all I could do was make a shaky gasping sound as I inhaled.

"Steady," Bigelow urged. "Breathe deeper. Slow your breaths down."

I kept on panting, but as Bigelow's voice grew softer my breaths grew deeper, and gradually the short gasps turned slower and steadier.

"That's it. Good. If you first control your body, then you can focus your mind."

"It...It's working," I said quietly as my breaths grew steady and more relaxed. "I'm calming down. Now how do I put out the fire?"

"You are already putting it out," Bigelow said.

"What?" I sputtered. My eyes flew back open and scanned all around the room. It was still filled with smoke, but the flames were fading. I looked at my RevealeR, and the waves of flame were down to a trickle. "How?"

"You have begun to tame your emotions. Now tell me, Will," Bigelow asked. "What does this 'Dunk' person do that upsets you?"

"What does he do? He picks on people!" I hissed at him fiercely. "He tortures guys like Gerald and me just for fun! And he has the nerve to act like he's not even doing anything wrong!"

"The flame has grown strong again," Bigelow interrupted.

I turned my eyes back to the RevealeR, and sure enough, waves of flame belched out of it. It was like an invisible fire-breathing dragon had come to life inside my flashlight. My jaw dropped, and I completely forgot what I had been saying.

"Calm yourself now, as you did before," Bigelow instructed. "Breathe deeply. Calm your body and focus your mind. Only then can the truth be revealed."

Well, though my eyes were burning and my cheeks were as red as tomatoes, it was actually easier to settle myself down the second time. I was able to deepen and slow my breaths more quickly, and my mind cleared as if a fog had lifted. As my rage dimmed, so too did the flame.

"You see it now, don't you Will?" Bigelow asked. I nodded dumbfoundedly.

"Yes. I understand now," I muttered softly. I lifted my RevealeR, and bright white light now flowed from its face. I stared at the clean, clear beam, and then looked to Bigelow.

"It was anger," I said. "Anger clouded my vision."

"That is correct," Bigelow said, smiling proudly with that big, toothy grin of his. "When you burn with anger, your rage is a flame that consumes you. That is what clouded your MonsterScope and corrupted the light of your RevealeR."

"You know," I growled as I turned and scowled at him. "You could have just told me that, instead of setting my room on fire."

Bigelow snickered.

"I could have simply explained this, it's true," he admitted. "But I'm afraid you must experience things a bit more bluntly to truly understand them. Anyway, fear not – look around you."

I looked around and gaped. The smoke, the burnt drapes, the charred bedposts...*everything*...everything was back as it was before.

"Everything...everything's back to normal," I gasped. "How...? The fire...The flames weren't real?"

"Oh, no," Bigelow said seriously, "The flames were quite real. But the fire that burns inside you destroys things much more precious and valuable than curtains. It wipes out judgment. It obliterates understanding. It devastates people's lives more surely than any inferno."

"And... and that's what kept me from solving the case?" I asked. Bigelow nodded.

"Yes. But putting aside your anger is just the beginning. To truly understand Duncan Williams, you must look past your own feelings and view the world through his eyes."

"But I don't want to see the world through his eyes! He's a bully! I don't even know why I should help him at all!"

I probably shouldn't have said that, but I couldn't help myself. Bigelow didn't answer at first, but then he said, "Will, to be a monster detective you must chose understanding and compassion over fear and anger. Even toward one who seems undeserving. That is the mark of a true hero."

"But I don't know if I *am* a true hero!"

"One does not *know*, Will. One *chooses*. You must choose who you are to be."

"But...but he's such a jerk! What can I do when he gets me mad like that? It's not like I can bring my Teddy with me to calm me down!"

Bigelow paused, and then scratched his chin.

"Calming yourself with controlled breathing is a good start," he said. "It is also useful to have actions or gestures that help to quiet your feelings. Try this..."

Bigelow put away his RevealeR and the held out his arms. He pulled back his overly long sleeves, exposing clawed, furry fingers.

"Make fists," he instructed, demonstrating with his own hairy hands. "Squeeze them tight."

I did just that, balling my hands so tight that the skin of my knuckles turned white.

"Good. Now open your hands. Release the tension from your fingers and your body," he said. "Feel your body relax. Next, bring your hands together slowly. Interlock your fingers and tap your chin with your index finger. Keep your breathing slow and steady."

I followed Bigelow's instructions, and even though it made me feel as ridiculous as the time I put my pajamas on backwards, it did make the tension pour out of my body.

"Very good, Will. But do not expect that composure will always come easily. It would be wise to practice this as much as possible."

"Kind of like taking batting practice before a ball game?"

"An apt analogy, yes."

I stared down at my hands, when suddenly a thought hit me.

"Hey! My mom does something like this! She did it the night I came back from Timmy Newsome's house, and again tonight!"

"Did she indeed?" Bigelow snickered. "And did it help?"

"No!" I growled. "Maybe she did it wrong. It didn't change anything. I got grounded for three days! "

"Are you sure it changed nothing?"

"What do you mean?"

"Well, did it occur to you how much worse your punishment might have been if your mother hadn't calmed herself?"

I tapped my fingers to my chin some more. "I hadn't thought of that."

"You know, change is a strange thing, Will," Bigelow mused. "You can look for it and look for it and see nothing. And yet slowly, in tiny little steps, things transform in ways you never imagined."

Chapter Eleven – Irritations

"Will! What on earth are you doing?"

Honestly, is there ever a good answer when your mom asks a question like that? But just so you know, what I was doing when my mother spied me at the breakfast table with my hands clasped together like a monk was practicing that *deep breathing to keep control over my emotions* thing that Bigelow taught me. I figured that if my calming ritual worked well enough to keep me from retching at the smell of my mom's artichoke and wheat germ waffles, it would work on pretty much anything.

"Um, nothing Mom," I answered quickly, breaking my hands apart and dropping them to my sides. "Just, um …nothing."

Her eyes narrowed, but then turned back to the stove.

"Go on and eat your breakfast," she said.

"I could sure use that flamethrower *now*," I grumbled to myself.

I stared at my plate, and checked out the latest experiment that had been poured into in my drinking glass, but then glanced back up at my mom. *It must have looked strange to her*, I thought, *seeing me sitting there looking like I was praying for deliverance* (which, given the smell of those waffles, I very nearly was). But then I remembered how I had seen her doing the same thing, and it made me wonder.

"Mom," I asked delicately, "Do you think I have a bad temper?"

There was a sudden snort from behind the newspaper perched in front of my dad's chair. My mom straightened, and turned to face me. She studied me carefully, but all she said was, "Perhaps...a bit."

The snort from behind the newspaper was followed by a loud snicker. I glared at the back of the paper for a moment, but then turned back to my mom.

"Do you think I get that from *you*?"

All of a sudden, the room went quiet. Like, *a pin-drop sounding like thunder* quiet. My dad even stopped rustling his paper. My mom's lips squeezed together so tightly that it looked like she was trying to crush an acorn in her mouth, but she answered quietly, "Maybe." She then glared over at my dad, but he remained silently hiding behind his newspaper. She slowly turned back to me and asked, "Why do you ask?"

I hesitated, but then I showed her my calming routine. My hands pressed close together, and my voice passed softly between my interlocked fingers.

"I saw you doing this," I said. "It's for helping you keep from losing your temper, isn't it?"

She stared at me for a moment, looking rather confused. Then she nodded. "Yes."

"Does it really work?"

For some reason, she looked over at my dad.

"*Some*times," she said quietly, and then turned back to the sink.

Jeannine missed the bus again that morning. I didn't panic like the last time of course, but in some ways, that made the trip even longer. I just sat in my seat quietly, without even getting into an argument with the bus driver. I felt invisible. The feeling lasted all the way into homeroom, where I sat almost in a daze until I felt a hard slap on the back of my head.

"Dreaming about your test tubes, Dorkenstein?"

I looked up to find Jacko McNulty standing over me. He snickered and swung his hand back as if he was going to hit me, but then ran his fingers through his hair instead. A snide smile spread across his face as he turned and walked down toward the back of the room.

"I'd grow eyes in the back of my head if I were you," he chuckled.

Well, if I needed something to make me practice controlling my emotions, this was the perfect chance. Just the sight of Jacko made me want to scream. I closed my eyes and balled my hands into fists, then slowly opened my palms and exhaled, bringing my fingers together and locking them like Bigelow showed me.

It worked, because I did start to feel less heated, but then things got weird.

Yes, weird even for me.

When I brought my fingers together, a strange calmness sprinkled over me, and I began to sense... *feelings* all around, just hanging in the air. I looked through the room, and suddenly realized that it was full of people. Of course, I know that homeroom is always full of people, but it suddenly felt like I had never noticed them before. As I glanced at their faces, an invisible web spun, connecting me with their thoughts and emotions, which flooded into me until it felt like I was drowning. My hands broke apart, and the feeling faded.

"Whoa," I muttered. "What was *that?*"

Just then, the bell rang, and I automatically got up and headed to class.

I didn't see Jeannine until math class that morning. She must have gotten to school late, because she was still carrying her jacket as she came bounding into the room just before the bell. She squealed and gave me an excited, wide-eyed look as she came toward my desk, but just then Mrs. McAllister coughed a loud 'Ahem' and announced, "Everyone in their seats, please." Jeannine sighed in disappointment, but we retreated to our seats at opposite ends of the room. After class, Jeannine rushed out of the room for some reason, but I caught up with her later on the way to lunch. She was at her locker, holding her books in one hand while prying the door open with the other (the door to her locker sticks, you see) when she saw me coming and began bouncing up and down in anticipation.

"So?" she asked as she hugged her books tightly. "Tell me everything! Did you make it to Duncan Williams' house?"

I nodded.

"Well?!! What happened?"

"Um, nothing much," I grumbled, looking down as I spoke. "I got there and began checking things out, but Dunk was being such a jerk that..."

...That when the monster showed up, smoke that was really fire came from my RevealeR making the monster impossible to see?? Somehow, I thought keeping the story simple would be better.

"...that I just couldn't find anything."

"That's it? You didn't find the monster? You didn't solve the case?"

"Hey, it was just my first visit! I didn't solve Timmy's case on the first day, but that worked out."

"Uh huh. Because the second time you went *I* was there to help you. What will you do now?"

"Well, I'm not even sure I'm going back. Dunk really didn't seem to want my help."

"He still has a monster," Jeannine said firmly. "He'll be back."

"Well then, aren't you going to come help me again when he does?"

"I can't, Will," she moaned. "I'm busy every minute of the day now! I have rehearsals, fittings, readings, makeup tests, you name it!"

"But...but I'm hunting monsters... you're not going to leave me to face them alone, are you?"

"Oh, don't make such a fuss," she chided. "I mean, what's the big deal? It's like I told you: The monsters won't really harm you, so just hang in there until you figure them out. You know you can do it."

"I...guess," I mumbled. "But it would be a lot easier if you were there to help me. After all, you defeated Gerald's monsters in just one night."

"To tell the truth," Jeannine snickered. "I don't know

which was harder to deal with: Gerald, or the monsters."

At that very moment a shrill, whiny voice pierced our ears like a spear of flame.

"Hey Jeannine," Gerald shrieked from down the hallway. "Wait up, wait up!"

Jeannine shuddered at the sound, but I just smirked at her. She scowled and said, "I take it back. I *do* know." Then she slammed shut her locker and hurried off. Just in time, as it turns out, because Gerald was on the spot in two seconds flat.

"Where's Jeannine?" he huffed, catching his breath.

"Um...bathroom," I said. Gerald frowned.

"She's ducking me, right?"

"No, of course not," I answered automatically. I couldn't help but try to spare Gerald's feelings, but once I told that lie, I started falling deeper into it. "She just has to go a lot. I think it's because girls have..."

"I'll bet she wouldn't have to go so much if I was as tall and strong as Duncan Williams," he hissed. "I've seen how she looks at him."

I looked at Gerald, his eyes brimming with anger and disappointment, and somehow felt that that strange wave of emotions passing into me again.

"Look, Gerald, you don't have to be a big, beefy jock to get someone to like you."

"Oh really? What should I do?"

"Well, if you really want people to like you, just..." I gulped loudly. "...just be yourself....."

At that very moment, Gerald sneezed, shooting flying boogers at me like a cannon. Then he wiped his nose on his sleeve.

"...only, you know, maybe a little less..."

Disgusting.

"...sloppy," I finished. "If you want to make a good impression, try cleaning yourself up a bit. Wash up. Comb you hair. Put your buttons in the right button holes. Tuck in your shirt...stuff like that."

"You really think so?" Gerald asked eagerly.

"Well, that would be a start, anyway. Why don't you go to the bathroom and...uh, straighten up?"

"OK," Gerald agreed, and then trotted off. I checked myself out, wiping off any bits of Gerald sticking to my clothes, and then headed to lunch. I found Jeannine in the cafeteria. Surprisingly, she was alone, seated in our old spot. As I came over to her, she looked over her shoulder to see if I was being followed.

"Don't worry," I assured her as I sat down. "It's safe to go back in the water, at least for a little while." Jeannine still looked around warily.

"Where's Gerald?"

"He's off in the bathroom, cleaning himself up so that he can earn your undying devotion. Speaking of that, where's Timmy?"

Jeannine glared at first, but then replied, "Guidance office. So, what did you use to get Gerald to leave you alone, and where can I buy some?"

"I just told him that people would like him better if he wasn't so clingy."

Jeannine blinked furiously, like something had just flown into her eye.

"You told Gerald how to get people to like him? *You*?"

"Um, yeah."

She shook her head as if I had just told her I'd planted a pencil to see if it would grow into a tree.

"Well, what else did you say?"

"I told him, you know, just be yourself."

"Be yourself? *Gerald*?"

"Yeah."

Jeannine glared at me.

"That is the stupidest thing I've ever heard!"

"Hey!" I protested. "It's what my parents tell *me* all the

time."

"Worst advice ever! What do they expect? That if you go on acting like a dork people will suddenly start liking it?"

I just sat there staring at her for a moment.

"Yeah, you're right," I finally agreed. "It never worked for me either. Where do grownups even come up with stuff like that, anyway?"

"I don't know. Maybe they watched too much TV when they were kids."

"I suppose. So then what can we do to help Gerald? He's convinced that as long as he has brains instead of muscles, he won't be able to make any friends."

"Well, we just have to show him that it isn't true. I mean, look at Drew Washburn. He's really smart, and he's got lots of friends, hasn't he?" she said, pointing over at the left corner of the cafeteria. There sat a very skinny, mousy-looking boy, with short, scruffy blond hair. He was clearly younger than everyone around him, a real stringbean sitting among lots of kids who were much bigger. He kind of reminded me of myself.

Except he had a whole tableful of friends that he was laughing and carousing with.

"Gee, go figure that he'd be over there, sucking up to all the popular kids. The ugly little worm!"

"Will! Are you …jealous?"

I sputtered, and sprayed pomegranate juice all over the table.

"Jealous? Of that little snot?"

"Oh, come on Will," Jeannine sighed exasperatedly. "Why do you hate him so? He's never done anything to you. You'd think the two of you would be great friends, what with you both being boy geniuses and all."

"I'll tell you why!" I barked. "That little brat just comes along and gets treated like a movie star. But when I won all those science awards, everyone treated me like a…well, like I had a disease or something! No one would talk to me! No one would sit with me at lunch! And now he show up and all of a sudden everyone *loves...*"

"What do you mean, no one?!" Jeannine shouted back, the sly smile suddenly crumbling. "Don't *I* count as someone? Haven't I been..."

"I didn't mean *you*," I interrupted impatiently. Jeannine folded her arms and glared at me. I sighed.

"Look," I said gently. "I'm sorry. Really. I know that you stood by me even when your friends teased you about hanging out with 'Little Jimmy Neutron'. You're more than just my partner. You're my best friend."

Jeannine's scowl softened, but she still eyed me suspiciously.

"You knew about us calling you 'Jimmy Neutron'?" she asked.

"Yeah," I answered. "Except I never found out who...wait, you said *us*. *You* called me that too?"

Jeannine squirmed a little. She pursed her lips and looked down, then started picking lint off her blouse.

"Actually, *I* was the one who came up with it," she said, looking back up at me.

"You?!" I sputtered. "You gave me that stupid nickname? Why...why would you *do* that?!"

"Well, I didn't know you at the time, Will," she explained quickly. "And the fact that you almost blew up the science lab on your very first day..."

"I did not blow it up!" I shouted angrily. "There was just a little smoke..."

"Which set off the alarm and gave the whole school an unplanned fire drill."

"Well, the flasks of chemicals were just sitting on the table when I got there. It looked like we were supposed to mix them..." I protested weakly.

Jeannine smirked.

"The point is, when word got out, you were famous. Everybody was talking about the little boy genius who nearly blew up the school. I just happened to be the one who came up with a clever nickname, and it stuck."

"Well, come up with a better one for Drew, OK?"

Jeannine laughed.

"Why don't *you* come up with something?" she suggested. "After all, you *are* the boy genius."

I gave Jeannine my best *this should burn you alive* stare, but she just giggled. When that didn't melt my scowl, she stomped on my foot.

"*Yooowwww,*" I moaned, grateful that she wasn't wearing her steel-toed boots. "What was that for?"

"That was to get that stupid scowl off your face," Jeannine said unapologetically. "You can thank me later."

"*Thank you?*" I growled.

"My mother always says that scowls put wrinkles under your eyes," she explained loftily.

"I see. So you shattering my toe was actually for my own good?" I scoffed.

"See?" Jeannine giggled. "You really *are* smart."

"All right, enough of all that! Are you going to help me with this case or not?"

"Well, I can't come with you, but maybe if you tell me about it I can help figure out what you missed."

"What I missed? I didn't miss anything! I just couldn't see Dunk's monster because my RevealeR and MonsterScope weren't working!"

"Oh, *please.* Only you, Will Allen, could be so observant and so oblivious at the same time."

"Oblivi…what?"

"Oblivious," Jeannine repeated in that snooty, you should know what I'm saying tone of voice. "It means you just don't notice things."

"Don't notice things?" I sputtered indignantly. "What are

you talking about?! I notice everything!"

"Really? Can you tell me what color Duncan's eyes are?"

"What? No!"

"They're blue. A deep, bold blue, like the ocean. Still think you notice everything?"

"That's doesn't count!" I roared. "Stuff like that doesn't help solve a case!"

"I think *I* know what helps solve a case," Jeannine said, her voice turning frosty. "In case you forgot, I just solved Gerald's case all by myself. And I did it in just one night."

"Sure. You got the easy one. But now you're too busy to..."

"Gerald's case was not easy! *You* couldn't have solved it! That's why the card picked me for the job. You have as much understanding for him as you do for a flatworm."

"What's a flatworm?"

"It's something you don't understand!"

"I understand Gerald just fine!" I protested. "I understand that he's a clingy little..."

"Ahem..." Jeannine suddenly coughed, her eyes darting from me at once.

"...booger-covered snot rag," I finished. "And just because you..."

But Jeannine was no longer listening. Her stare was fixed upon a spot directly behind me.

"Um, I should really look behind me, shouldn't I?"

I turned around, and there stood Gerald, a look of horror and betrayal mixed upon his face. I turned back to Jeannine and growled, "*This* is the one time you don't stomp on my foot?"

Jeannine didn't speak, she just motioned in Gerald's direction. I turned back to Gerald to apologize.

"Look, Gerald, I didn't really mean 'snot rag', I was just..." I began, but he had already turned and was headed away.

"Gerald, wait!" I called out. "I...I was, um...misquoted..."

But he exited through the lunch room door, turned the corner and was out of sight. A sudden ache throbbed in my temples, and I rubbed them vigorously.

"Great," I moaned. "So much for new friends."

"Misquoted?" Jeannine chided. "Is that the best you could come up with?"

"It was just the word that popped into my head!"

"Well, as usual, when it comes to English, your head pops in all the wrong directions. No wonder I beat you on the last three tests."

Oh, did I mention that Jeannine is insanely competitive about grades? She wants the best grades like Cruella DeVille wants puppies.

"Great! You're beating me at English!" I said. "That makes one class out of six!"

No, I *wasn't* being competitive too. But facts are facts.

"Well, of course, no one beats little Jimmy Neutron at science..." she chimed. "Oh, except for Drew, who's what...a year younger than you?"

"Don't call me 'Jimmy Neutron'!" I yelled. My cheeks grew hotter, until I could feel the heat from them burning my eyes like they were marshmallows held over a grill. I glared at her.

"You're really enjoying pushing my buttons today, aren't you?" I muttered.

"Maybe a little," she confessed without a hint of shame. "But it would certainly be more fun if it wasn't so easy."

Chapter Twelve – Do Overs

OK, give Jeannine credit: she's pretty sharp when it comes to dealing with people. At least, when she wants to be. Not only can she annoy me or get me to do what she wants whenever she feels like it, she had Duncan Williams figured out too. He did come looking for my help once more, just like she said he would. But this time he decided to be sly about it.

"You didn't tell me," whispered a deep, steady voice that crept up behind me as I walked down the corridor after lunch. I turned to look, but Dunk kept going, moving into me and pushing me around the corner and out of sight of the people in the hallway.

"Didn't tell you what?" I demanded as I pulled loose and faced him squarely. My fists balled up and I crouched slightly as though bracing for an attack, but I stopped when I saw his eyes. Their color was deep blue like Jeannine said, but they were sunken, fearful, and lined with dark circles like those of an old lady.

"You didn't tell me," he said. "You didn't tell me that it would get worse."

"Worse? Worse how?"

Dunk hesitated, but then pulled up his left sleeve to the elbow, revealing a long stretch of taped gauze.

"Told my dad I got these working in the garage," he said.

"He went nuts…said I must be crazy, jeopardizing my future by playing around with some old engine parts." He peeled back the gauze. There were four deep scratches gouged diagonally across his forearm.

"The monster came back," he said. "But it didn't just stand there like before. It came after me, and grabbed my arm. I was barely able to pull free and get to the light switch. When I turned on my lamp, it disappeared. Then I turned off the light, and it was right there again. After that, I left the light on all night."

"So?" I said gruffly. "So you sleep with the light on from now on. What do you want from me? I'm useless, remember?"

Dunk looked away. His head shook back and forth.

"It's going to keep getting worse, isn't it?"

"Probably."

He nodded in a herky-jerky kind of way, and then said to the wall, "I need to do something."

"Well, good luck," I hissed, and began to walk away. Dunk stepped in front of me, and grabbed me by the shoulders. I tore myself free.

"You can't frighten me or order me to do what you want!" I growled. "I thought you'd have figured that out by now!"

"Then what can I do?" His eyes, those haunted blue eyes, were pleading.

"You can *ask*." I replied firmly. "You can ask real nice. Maybe even say please."

"Please?" he repeated, as though I was talking in some foreign language.

"*Pretty please with sugar on top* is even better."

"What?" he spat. "I'm not some stinking beggar! I'm Duncan Williams! I'm the one who gets it done!"

"Look, I'm not going to mess around with you, Dunk! Do you want my help or not?"

Dunk threw his arms in the air, and grabbed his head like it was about to burst. Slowly, his hands slid across his shoulders and he rubbed his arms like he was in a meat locker.

"All right," he whispered. "I need your help. Will you do it? Will you help me?"

I just stared at him.

"...*Please*?" he added gingerly, as though it caused him great pain to speak. I have to admit, I kind of enjoyed making Dunk grovel like that, but then I felt ashamed for enjoying it.

"All right, I'll do it," I finally answered. But you have to promise that this time you'll do what I tell you. No arguments – agreed?"

Dunk looked away and fidgeted, but finally muttered, "OK." Then he looked back up at me. "So then, can you do it tonight? I can't take another night like last night."

"Sure. If I can survive the trip to your house, that is. My bicycle is only fit for a toddler, and it tries to maim me every time I ride."

"So why don't you just get another one? That's what I do. I've got half a dozen bikes that I've outgrown sitting in my garage."

"Well, goody for you," I grumbled. Then it went quiet.

"So, you're coming?" Dunk confirmed.

I nodded. "I'll see you tonight."

I'll spare you the details about how I made my way to Dunk's house that evening. It's enough to say that it involved another generous dose of aggravation, frustration, and pain. I arrived at his door with some fresh scrapes and scratches, a tear in my pants, and my bicycle seat in my hands. I used the padded end of the seat to knock on the door.

"Yah?" Dunk's dad called out from within. "Who's dere,

mon?"

"It's me, Mr. Williams. Will Allen," I yelled through the door. A loud stomping sound followed, until I heard the latches on the door being unlocked, and then it creaked open. Mr. Williams stood in the doorway, and checked me out head to toe.

"Wha happen to you?" he asked. "You in a accident?"

"Um, car problems," I answered. Mr. Williams scratched his head.

"You drive a car?"

"No. That's the problem. May I come in?"

Mr. Williams pointed me up to Dunk's room and then headed back to the living room, where he slumped down into the easy chair in front of the TV. I looked back at him as I made my way up the stairs. It was hard to believe that this was the same man who stood so straight and proud in the picture on Dunk's wall. When I got to Dunk's door, it swung open before I could even knock.

"About time!" Dunk growled, but then he checked me out with the same up and down scan his father had.

"What happened to you?" he asked. "Were you fighting some other monsters before you got here?"

I thought of my booby-trap of a bicycle and answered, "Something like that. Now, are you ready to get on with it?"

Dunk nodded nervously, and then moved aside to let me enter. As I stepped into his room, I noticed right away that it was different somehow.

"Did you move things around?"

"No. Why?"

I looked all around, and the furniture, the decorations, and everything else were the same, but the *feel* was different. The room seemed uncomfortably small, and the colors of the walls and hangings seemed dark and muddy.

"It was over there this time," Dunk announced, pointing to the far side of his desk. "The monster appeared over there by the wall."

I walked on over and checked it out. Below on the floor beside the desk was a tin wastebasket, and as my gaze lifted, I saw that I was standing in front of the photo of Dunk's championship team. There before my eyes were the smug, smiling faces of Dunk, Jacko, Truck, and the other boys who had menaced me in the bathroom, all happily sharing in a moment of glorious triumph. I started to get angry again, I mean, it's just so unfair, you know?

"Hey, you spacing or what?" Dunk called out, clapping me on the back. I glared at him, but then turned back to the photo.

"Do you think this has something to do with the monster?" he went on. I paused a moment, but then reminded myself that I was there to find the monster, so I pulled out my MonsterScope and set about examining the area.

"Ah, no...not again," I grumbled when I realized that the glass was foggy and unreadable once more.

"What is it?"

"Nothing...nothing..." I replied. I remembered what Bigelow had said about anger clouding my vision, so I did that hand gesture thing to try and clear my mind. I think it was working too, because after I relaxed my fists and brought my hands together, the scope began to grow clearer. But then...

"What stupid freakazoid thing are you doing now?"

The blood instantly rushed to my cheeks, and I felt flames licking at the back of my eye sockets, but I kept my breaths deep and steady.

"You know," I said calmly, though my teeth were clenched, "You only make it harder for me to help you when make fun of me."

Dunk hesitated. He tilted his head and stared at me strangely, but then spat out, "Oh, get over it! You think you're the only one who's ever been made fun of? It happens to everyone!"

I closed my eyes and tried to keep my breaths steady.

"If that's your idea of an apology, I…wait…" My eyes suddenly sprung open. "You – are you saying you've been made fun of too? *You*?"

"Oh don't act so innocent!" Dunk growled. "You were probably one of them! Following me around – calling me 'Dorky Duncan' or 'Duncan Donut'. I hated going to school all through first grade!"

I just stared at him.

"I've only been here since second grade," I said. "That was when my family moved here."

Dunk continued glaring at me.

"Then you probably did it to someone at your old school," he said. "That's just what people do. Everyone makes fun of someone."

"I would never…" But then I stopped. The image of Gerald Hoffsteadler, his face a mix of horror and betrayal, flashed into my brain. I looked down.

"That doesn't make it right," I whispered.

"Yeah, well, like I said: get over it."

I looked back up at him, not certain of what I was going to say, when suddenly my MonsterScope turned warm in my hand.

"What…?" I muttered distractedly, looking down at it as it hung in my grasp.

Then I gasped.

"What?" Dunk called out, suddenly sounding concerned. "What is it?"

"My MonsterScope," I said. "It…it's clear!"

Dunk rolled his eyes and groaned.

"So?" he hissed. "How does that help? I thought you finally *found* something!"

"You don't understand," I explained. "I can see through it now. Before it was…"

But then I stopped. I remembered that I hadn't told Dunk about my scope going dark, and I wasn't going to confess that *now*, so…

"Well, let's start looking," I said, and I raised the glass and looked around the room. Then I gasped again.

"Now what?" Dunk groaned.

"Um, nothing," I answered. "Just hiccups."

It wasn't hiccups. It was what I saw in the MonsterScope. Looking through it, the whole room became so clear that it made my head hurt, like I was a nearsighted person putting on reading glasses that were too strong. But not all of the room had become clear: parts were still foggy, like the lens was dirty in spots. Only I quickly realized it wasn't the glass that was foggy. No matter where I moved or what angle I looked from, certain objects remained fuzzy, including Dunk's wastebasket, his wall pictures, and a small charm hanging from a thin gold chain that was draped over a picture frame on his nightstand. I went over to inspect the charm.

"What is this?" I asked, picking it up to examine it more closely.

"Put that down!" Dunk cried out furiously. "Don't you go fooling around with my stuff!"

"I have to check out everything!" I shot back angrily. "Now do you want my help or not?"

Dunk squirmed and twitched, and scratched, though his eyes remained fierce.

"That…that's got nothing to do with monsters!" he growled.

"You can't know that for sure," I maintained. "For all we know, this could actually be an important clue."

Dunk looked away, and his squirming grew more animated.

"It…it's called an Ankh. It was my mother's, OK?" he finally blurted. "She gave it to me before…"

And then his squirming stopped, and he slumped like a puppet that had its strings cut.

"It was my mother's," he whispered.

I looked over at Dunk, then down at the charm. Somehow, the blurry haze around it had faded, and I saw it clearly. It was a shiny gold figure 8 without the bottom, but the gold was worn and tarnished in spots, like someone had rubbed it hard over and over again. My gaze then shifted down to the picture on the nightstand where the chain had rested. In it, a young woman, fair-skinned with long black hair, smiled broadly as she held up a scrawny toddler whose hands pushed playfully against her face. There was no sense of fear or even anger coming from it: the photo radiated warmth, and yet also pain and sadness. But there was nothing monster*ish* about it at all. Just to be sure, I scanned the photo carefully with my MonsterScope, and then looked back up at Dunk.

"You're right," I concluded. "This has nothing to do with the monsters."

It remained quiet for a bit, and I set out in silence to busy myself examining more of the room, searching for clues.

To tell you the truth, I was feeling a bit ashamed – here I was, trying to prove what a professional detective I was, and I hadn't even noticed that Dunk had no mother. Looking back, the evidence had been there all along, but for some reason I just hadn't taken it in. Now, I could have probed for more details about that, but something deep inside me told me that it was rightly left alone. Instead, I lifted my MonsterScope and continued searching.

"Show me again where the monster was."

Dunk pointed once more at the far corner of his desk. I walked over and checked out the area again, this time using my MonsterScope. Through it, the walls grew darker, but Dunk's team photo was bright, almost glowing. And in the odd clarity that the light provided, it appeared as if the photo was full of wrinkles, as though it had been crumpled up and then uncrumpled. I stepped closer to look it over more carefully, and noticed something strange: the expressions on the faces of the boys in the picture had *changed*. Some still wore the same happy smiles as before, but others, including Dunk, looked fearful. As I looked over the whole team, joy was still clearly visible in some boys' eyes, but others now displayed terror, relief, sadness, and in some cases, rage. I lowered my scope, and all the faces looked happy once more.

"Well I'll be..." I muttered. "I wonder what that's all about?"

But then I gasped, because my MonsterScope, which was carelessly pointed downward, suddenly had something bright shining through its lens. Staring down through the glass at the wastebasket, I saw something glowing along the sides of the pail. As I bent down closer, I thought I saw something rustle in the dark recesses of the basket, and gingerly reached my hand inside. My fingers slowly probed deeper until...

"Eeeeeuuuuwwwww!" I cried, pulling my hand out quickly. "There's nothing but snotty tissues in here!"

"Well, what did you expect?" Dunk protested. "It's a trash can!"

I quietly snarled, but then shifted my gaze to the outside of the can. Through the lens, there were sets of glowing marks that looked like paw prints. Lots of them.

"Um, Dunk. You don't have a dog, do you?"

"No. My dad's allergic."

"A bear then?"

Dunk chuckled. "No. Why?"

"Um...No reason."

The marks traveled down the side of the can and continued across the floor. There seemed to be dozens of different kinds, some with three toes and others with as many as seven, all moving in the same direction. I followed the prints, and the tracks led right up to Dunk's closet, and disappeared under the door.

"Something…" I whispered. "Something is in there…"

I carefully turned the knob on the closet door, but no sooner had the bolt unlatched when the door thrust itself open and something dark and fetid jumped out and smothered me.

"Yaaahhh!" I cried as I struggled with the smelly mass. But Dunk just laughed. I finally pulled part of my attacker away from my face and saw that there were words written on

it: 'Property of Ashford Middle School Athletic Department'.
I held it up.

"A T-shirt?" I puzzled. "I was attacked by..."

But just then, I jumped back as an entire stack of t-shirts,
shorts, and dirty underwear collapsed on me, and as they did
a football fell out and bounced across the floor. I stood
staring at it, but Dunk just grabbed it and flung it back into
the closet on top of the pile of clothes.

"Don't worry about the mess," Dunk, chuckled. "I don't
think you have anything to fear from my dirty laundry."

"Are you kidding? Anyone with a sense of smell should
be terrified..." But then I stopped, because I noticed a hazy
glow through the lens of my MonsterScope. I pressed it
close to my eye and I looked carefully into Dunk's closet.
The glow radiated throbs of energy from its source, which sat
upon a throne of dirty laundry.

"That football..." I stuttered, dropping the glass to my
side in shock.

"What about it?"

I lifted my scope once more to be sure.

"It...it's a monster."

Utter silence suddenly fell upon us. Then Dunk broke out
in a fit of laughter. He laughed so hard that he doubled over
and slid down to the floor.

"Good...good one..." he chortled as he held his sides to
keep from bursting. But I ignored him. My MonsterScope
was pointed into Dunk's closet at the football perched upon
the stack of dirty clothes, and through the lens, there was a
pulsing, kaleidoscopic glow swirling around the ball,
growing brighter as I watched. As the glow grew intense,
everything surrounding it grew darker, as though the football
was sucking all the light in the area into itself. Shadows
swelled within the closet and began to spread. I lowered my
MonsterScope, and even to the naked eye the darkness was
clearly growing.

That's a sure sign of a monster at work. But Dunk seemed completely oblivious.

Yes, that's that word Jeannine used. We all know what it means now, right?

"Could you give me a hand here?" he laughed as he extended his hand for me to help him up. But before I could grab him, the shadows from the closet advanced across the room, completely covering him.

"Hey, what happened to the light?" Dunk's voice echoed through the sudden, smothering darkness that was so complete that I couldn't see my own hand, much less Dunk's. I reached out to him, and my fingers closed on a hand that hung in the void.

"Gotcha!" I called out.

But the hand in my grasp was cold, hairy, and slimy, and as I probed further, I found the fingers were tipped by long, sharp talons.

"Uh, Dunk…have you trimmed your nails lately?" I whispered into the darkness where the shadow fell.

Unfortunately Dunk's voice called back from the other direction.

Chapter Thirteen – Beneath the Veil

"What? What did you say?" Dunk replied. I instantly dropped my grip on the hand in the darkness and scurried back.

"Um, Dunk? I have some good news and some bad news..."

"Really?" he called out. "What's the good news?"

"I think I've finally found your monster," I answered.

"That's the *good* news?" he hissed. "Then what's the bad news?"

"It...well, it looks like he's found *us*."

At that very moment, a ferocious howl pierced the darkness. Even as I held my ears against that horrid sound, it was followed by a series of high-pitched roars and growls.

"Uh oh," I whispered. "Dunk, has anything like this ever happened before?"

Dunk didn't answer.

"Dunk?!" I shouted.

"No...no..." I heard him mumble from a spot to my right. I pulled out my RevealeR, but hesitated before turning it on, seeing as how the last time I used it my room turned into a giant weenie roast. I bit my lip, and then flicked the switch and pointed the beam in the direction of Dunk's voice. Thankfully, what poured out wasn't flame, but it wasn't normal light either. The rays that came out were weak, slightly greenish, and sort of bubbly like the fizz from a soda, but they weren't so weak that I couldn't spy Dunk standing out against the growing shadows. I moved closer to him and then turned and pointed the light directly into the space where the monster's hand had been. I swung the RevealeR slowly back and forth until a sharp gleam, like the reflection from a raised knife, reflected back. Waving the beam up and down, bits of a silhouette came into view: a rounded shoulder here, a long torso there, and then another shiny flash reflected back at my eyes from pointy, glistening claws scratching at the air. There wasn't much more to see: the entire figure was blanketed in a darkness my fizzy beam could not penetrate, whose base, like flowing lava, slowly spread across the floor.

"This is it," I whispered as I crept closer. "Come on!"

"Are you crazy?" Dunk hollered as he grabbed my shoulder and pulled me back. "Didn't you see what that thing did to me?" He yanked up his sleeve and showed me again the gashes on his arm.

"It just wants to scare you Dunk," I said, pulling loose.

"*Scare* me?" Dunk shouted, stumbling as he tried to back away. "It wants to eat me alive!"

"No it doesn't! Monsters feed on your fear. But you need to face this thing if you want to defeat it."

But as I argued, an invisible yet determined force began puling us both toward the monster. I looked down, and saw that the waves of darkness that flowed from the dark figure were swirling around our feet like an ocean tide, drawing us closer to the motionless, blanketed form.

"It's sucking us in!" Dunk cried.

"Let it!" I shouted. "We need to get closer. We need to find out your monster's true form!"

"How? It's covered in that...that big slimy blanket!"

I turned to Dunk and said, "Then we need to see what it's hiding. We need to look under that... that *shroud*."

I stepped forward and reached gingerly to grasp the edge of the shadowy cloak, but my hand passed through it like smoke. My fingers reached deeper, but just as they touched something, the figure within suddenly turned and roared at me fiercely, and the dark tide that was drawing me toward the monster reversed itself. It whipped at me like a hurricane, forcing me back and blowing my hat clean off my head. I stumbled, and then picked up my hat as the figure turned away again and was still.

"Um, I mean *you* need to look under it," I corrected.

"Me?" Dunk protested. "You're the..."

"Oh, let's not start *that* again! This is something you've got to do!"

"Then what am I paying you for?"

"Funny, but now that you mention it, *you haven't paid me anything*!"

"Don't you worry! I always pay my debts!"

"Great! Do you always keep your word, too? Because you agreed to do whatever I told you!"

Dunk gulped hard. For a moment, he looked like he was

going to cry, but then his face twisted into a tight grimace. He balled his fists, and slowly approached the monster. There was no movement under the shroud as he drew closer, but Dunk's hand shook violently as he reached to touch it.

"Here goes nothing," he moaned. Then, in one motion, his hand grabbed at the top corner of the dark, wriggling sheet, and pulled. Nothing happened, as the sheet seemed to melt right through Dunk's fingers.

"Come on, just do it!" I cried.

"I'm trying!" Dunk hissed back. "It just slipped!"

"Well, grip it tighter!

"Gee, thanks, Jimmy Neutron! Like I couldn't have thought of that myself!"

"Don't call me Jimmy Neutron!" I scowled at Dunk, who glared back, but then reached for the sheet of darkness and grabbed at it again. Once more, it melted through his hand.

"It won't come off!" Dunk bellowed. "Now what?"

I frowned, but then brought my hands together and tapped my fingers to my lips to clear my mind.

"This...this shroud of darkness is hiding the monster, keeping us from seeing what form it's taking. What we need is for the light of truth to help us to see through it."

"Oh, great!" Dunk muttered. "And where are we going to get that?"

"That's the power of my RevealeR," I explained, lifting my special flashlight for him to see. "With a little understanding, its light should be able to break through the shadows. But I *don't* understand. The monster I saw was a football. Why are you scared of a football?"

"I'm not! Only *babies* are scared of the ball!"

"Only babies...?" I muttered. Without realizing it, Dunk had given me a crucial clue. *When he was a child*, I thought, *Dunk must have been afraid of getting hit by the ball just like anyone else, even if he isn't anymore.*

"This is like my toilet-monster," I whispered.

"Say what?"

"This isn't your true monster," I explained. "This is a decoy we have to get past to find your hidden beast – the secret fear that powers all of your monsters."

"You had to get past a toilet?"

"It was a decoy! Monsters take the form of anything that scares us, even old fears that we've forgotten. Our true monsters hide behind ones like this to keep from being discovered."

"Your monster was a *toilet*?"

"*Yours* is a football. Or at least it was! But to conquer it, we need to see what's under that shroud!"

"How? I can't get it off, and you can't even get close!"

"We need to understand. Understanding is what reveals the truth."

"But...*how*? Dunk protested. "How can we understand what's under there if we don't even know what it is?"

"We *do* know what it is!" I insisted. "It's something that scared you when you were a little kid. Can't you remember anything that used to frighten you?"

"I...uh, well..." Dunk stuttered. His eyes suddenly drifted and lost focus, like he was staring at a faraway lighthouse. At that very moment, another loud howl pierced through the shadows.

"Hoooowwoouuuuwww..." cried the monster. The sound echoed and lingered, but I noticed as it faded that another sound began filling the air in its place.

"That sound..." I whispered. "It sounds like...like *circus* music."

I looked back at Dunk, but he was crouched, his eyes squeezed tightly shut, covering his ears and thrashing around like someone was blowing a bugle at his head.

"You remembered something, didn't you?" I called out. "You remembered something that scared you!"

But Dunk didn't answer, unless you count moaning like a

baby with a belly ache as a form of speech, so I stared right into his eyes and shouted, "You know what's under there! You just have to face it! Pull off the shadow covering the monster and look it in the eye!"

Dunk twisted up like a pretzel, shook his head, and shuddered violently, but then grabbed the shroud in one quick motion and tugged.

Instantly, several things happened. The shadowy blanket slid from the top of the monster, revealing a huge, hideously deformed head with massive, fire-red eyes. The dark current retreated, and the shroud of shadows turned liquid in Dunk's hand, pouring through his fingers and reforming around the monster like a robe, covering its body and forming a hood over its head. And worst of all, the monster came alive, raising its arms and then turning and roaring at us so fiercely that it blew Dunk away like a twig in a tornado and sprayed spit all over both of us. And all the while the circus music continued to play.

"Oh, gross!" I whined as the monster's gooey spray splattered my coat, hat, and face. "Remind me to wash with disinfectant when this is all over."

As I wiped the slime from my chin, I lifted the beam from my RevealeR until it fell upon the monster's face. Its huge red eyes extended from the top of its mottled grey forehead down past a bulbous purple nose all the way to the monster's ear to ear black and red lips. Huge tufts of bright orange hair, tangled and matted like cotton balls, surrounded the head, and the mouth was frozen in a vacant grin.

"This is what you were afraid of? A...a circus clown?"

"They're creepy-looking, OK?" he shouted as he straightened back up from where he landed. "Just...just do your job and make it go away!"

"I keep telling you it doesn't work like that, Dunk!" I shouted back. "You have to face your monster to conquer it!"

At just that moment, the monster roared again, and I put my hand in front of my face to block the spit. Dunk spun and

cowered as he was blown all the way back to the wall, but I
squinted through my spit-sprayed fingers at the monster's
face. Strangely, even though it was roaring, the monster's
jaws were still frozen like plaster.

"Wait...Something - something's not right here..."

"Well, duh, genius-boy!" Dunk replied, straining against
the winds pressing him against the wall. "What gave you the
first clue?"

"No, I mean there's something not right about this
monster. It seems...*fake*. Those eyes and lips look...*painted*
on...Not like a real monster at all."

Just as those words fell from my lips, the air between me
and Dunk suddenly became alight.

"Hey, your flashlight-thing...it just turned brighter!"

I lifted the RevealeR up in front of my face, and sure
enough, its beam was stronger, and had turned slightly blue.

"What the..." I mumbled. "But...but that only happens
when I understand something. And all I said was..."

My gaze shifted from my RevealeR to the frozen, rigid
face of the monster.

"You're a fake..." I muttered, and the light grew stronger still and the flow, though still bubbly, turned steadier.

And with that, I turned the RevealeR's beam to the clown's face. A cracking sound suddenly rose above the circus music, and fractures began to form around the edges of its hairline. There were several more cracking noises, and then the monster's whole face *snapped right off its head.*

"It...it..." Dunk stuttered. "...It was a mask!"

The clown-face slid from the monster's head and fell to the floor. The matted orange hair surrounding the head turned dark, straight, and thick, as a short snout capped by a large, triangle shaped black nose poked out from under the hood. Below the snout hung rows of sharp fangs, big as steak knives, and narrow black eyes that were cold and without pity gleamed from within the hood.

"That...that's him?" Dunk asked weakly. "Is that the true face of my monster?"

"Could be. Or it could be another decoy," I replied, being careful to keep my eyes, and the beam of my RevealeR, pointed squarely on the monster. "Either way, now that you're facing the truth about your monster, it will grow smaller, and its power over you will be broken."

And indeed, as the cascading bubbles of blue light from my RevealeR continued to pour onto the beast, its head began to lower and sink into the cloak. I smiled in triumph, but then Dunk grabbed my arm and started shaking.

"You've got to stop!" he shouted. "Stop it! If you don't that thing will kill us both!"

"No it won't!" I assured him. Look, it's shrinking! It's getting weaker by the second."

"No it's not!" Dunk insisted. "It's crouching! It's getting ready to spring at us!"

"Look, who's the monster detective here?" I grumbled, as I turned and glared at him. "I think I know when..."

But I never got to finish my sentence.

Chapter Fourteen – The Master of the Beasts

OK, score one for Dunk, because while my head was turned, the monster jumped out from under the cloak and came flying through the air at us. Distracted and disbelieving, I stood there, a sitting duck, as dagger-like claws soared right at my throat.

"Duck!" Dunk shouted, pushing me down as the beast flew right over our heads. As it passed, I felt a searing pain across my shoulder, but I didn't have time to pay any mind to it before I crashed, face first, into the floor. I quickly looked up, but the monster had vanished into the darkness. I lifted my RevealeR to search Dunk's room to find where it had gone, and my jaw dropped in shock.

You see, we weren't in Dunk's room anymore. Or at least, that's not what it looked like. In the RevealeR's light, our setting had changed: within the gloomy shadows that surrounded us there now floated a series of steel bars that circled us to form a cage, with several waist-high stools spaced within. Far deeper into the murky darkness, there appeared to be the outline of stadium seats filled with a crowd of people.

"We…" I stuttered. "We're trapped!"

Just as I said that, another roar erupted, only this one was high-pitched, almost squeaky, and came from where the cloak had been. I lifted my head and looked back. The cloak was still there, floating in front of us even though the monster was no longer inside.

"What?" I wondered out loud as I began to rise back up from the floor. "What's this all about?"

"Stay down!" Dunk instructed, grabbing me from behind. "I'm not sure I'll be able to keep that thing from tearing your head off next time!"

"Um, thanks," I said weakly. "But you know, I didn't need for you to..."

But as I spoke, Dunk's eyes focused on something directly over my shoulder, and grew wide with terror.

"Look out!" he shouted, and shoved me down once more. My face slammed onto the floor again, making my teeth rattle and my head spin.

"Oooowww!" I hissed, rubbing my chin as I pushed my head back up from the ground. I looked over at Dunk angrily.

"This is ridiculous!" I grumbled. "I may be safe from the monsters, but you saving me is going to kill me!"

But Dunk's eyes were following something flashing through the air above us. I lifted my chin to see that a *second* beast had sprung from the cloak. As I watched from the ground, it leapt through the air and then pranced around the room in a jittery, herky-jerky way.

"What..." I wondered out loud. "What is that *smell*?" I followed the smelly monster's movements with my light as it stepped up to one of the stools and climbed on, and then I spotted the first monster sitting on the stool right beside it. Seeing them side by side, I noticed that they were very different beasts. The first looked very much like a lion but for the slimy, glistening fur, the golden mane cut flat across the top of its head, and the talons that were more like the claws of a bird. The second was smaller and thinner with a pointed, mousy snout that covered two long, thin fangs jutting down from the front of its jaw. Its black and grey fur was spotted and short, and spiked ears jutted out of the long, black hair on the top of its head. The spike-eared monster growled its squeaky roar at the lion-monster, which hissed a quiet growl in return, and then the second monster turned away and roared into the empty air. Suddenly, more beastly howls filled the room in reply.

"What...what are those *things* doing?" Dunk said.

"I don't know," I answered as the howls of unseen wild beasts grew louder, nearer. "But it sounds like that spike-eared monster is crying out for..."

The moment that thought hit my head, I spun around and flashed my RevealeR back at the cloak.

"...For his friends," I finished. And sure enough, the jaws of another wild beast were already flying at our heads.

"Down!" I shouted, shoving Dunk to the floor just as the monster's glistening fangs cut through the air where his head had been.

"Hey!" Dunk protested as he pushed himself up from the floor. "Watch who you're..."

But before he could finish his words, he yelped and

dropped back to the floor as more strange monsters, one after another, burst forth from the inner folds of the shadowy shroud.

Well not *strange* monsters really – actually they were pretty ordinary as monsters go: a seven foot tall T-Rex with a thick gold collar (ho-hum), a grey-furred werewolf chewing on his own thick tongue (been there, done that), and a seven-fingered Saber-toothed tiger wearing knickers. Pretty unimaginative, if you ask me. Anyway, they all pranced across the room to join the lion and spike-eared monsters, and then sat on the stools beside them. When they were all in place and every stool was filled, the monsters leaned their heads back and roared together.

I covered my ears, but Dunk was beside himself. He shook and shivered as he lay upon the floor, and his head kept spinning in every direction. As he writhed, the monsters grew even larger.

"Oh my god!" he muttered through chattering teeth. "Oh my god, what am I going to do? They're going to eat me alive!"

"Relax, Dunk," I said, putting my hand on his shoulder as I knelt beside him, trying to calm him down. "Monsters won't actually hurt you. They just want to scare you, so that they can feed off of your fear…"

But at just that moment, the roaring stopped, and the monsters' heads all turned to face us. The cold, dark eyes of the spike-eared monster met mine, and he let out a low, menacing snarl. Immediately, the other began to growl as well, and the room filled with a rumbling like race cars at the starting line. But even though they were gunning their engines, something seemed to be holding them back.

"They're going to eat me alive," Dunk whispered again, pulling away and shaking off my hand. "We're doomed!"

"We're not doomed!" I hissed irritably. "In fact, they don't even seem that interested in us. It's like they're waiting for something…"

"Or some*one*..." Dunk muttered. I glared at him.

"Someone? These are *your* monsters, Dunk! Who would they be waiting for?"

Dunk just stared blankly, but right then several loud snapping sounds pierced the air. The monsters squirmed and roared like someone had put ants in their pants.

And no, that hasn't ever happened to me, but I hear it's very uncomfortable. Anyway, the snapping sounds kept erupting, and monsters were growing frenzied. Their heads spun in one direction, then the other, and they waved their paws wildly in the air. Finally, Spike (that's the name I gave the spike-eared monster – yeah, I do stuff like that) roared his squeaky growl at the others, who stirred, and began stepping down from their stools. Before they even reached the ground, another loud snap rang out, and they all retreated back to their places, but for Spike. He squirmed and roared, then suddenly sprang from his stool, claws extended, right at Dunk.

"Dunk, look out!" I shouted, but before I could even get the words out, the monster was upon him. Its claws landed square on Dunk's shoulders as he sat frozen on the floor, and drove him back to the ground. The monster leaned its pointy fangs within inches of his face and howled, and then a low, distant roaring echoed around us.

"No! Get off!" Dunk screeched, trying to fend off the monster with his arms. I shot forward to try and pull the monster off of him, but at that very moment, another loud snapping sound pierced the air. Spike looked up, and then leaped from Dunk in the direction of the noise.

"Dunk!" I shouted as I grabbed his shoulders and pulled him back to a sitting position. "Are you all right?"

But he pushed me away.

"Where..." he gasped. "Where did he go?"

And we both turned in the direction that the monster had leapt. I pointed my light, and found Spike crouched in front of the floating shroud, which billowed like a strong wind was blowing it. From beneath the rippling shroud, a voice rang out.

"Return to your proper place," boomed a deep, hollow voice. Spike growled, but then there was another snap, and he backed away.

"You shall do as I say," thundered the ghostly voice. "For I am your master. The master of the beasts." Dunk stiffened as the voice filled the room, and the monsters bowed their heads, but for Spike. He snarled at the shrouded figure, and his head shook and twitched. In response, one of the sleeves of the cloak arose, and a slimy, clawed hand emerged, which reared back and unfurled a long, sharp whip from within its grasp. The hand shook, and the whip came to life, dancing like a charmed snake. It rippled and flew through the air, snapping at the heels of Spike, who stepped back, and snarled again.

"So that's where that snapping sound was coming from!" Dunk realized. "But what does this all mean?"

"Somehow, that whip must be the key to you defeating the monsters," I surmised. "That's what that...that *beastmaster* is using to keep them under control."

"Does he really have them under control, though?" Dunk asked. "Because that *jackal* looks like he's about to..."

And even as Dunk spoke, Spike shook off the last crack of the whip and reared up.

"Oh, no..." Dunk whispered just as Spike crouched, and then sprang right into the opening in the cloak. He disappeared into the hood for a second, but then backed his way out, tail first, dragging something along with him.

"No! No! You must obey!" the haunting voice of the beastmaster cried out as he was slowly pulled from behind the dark veil of the shroud. He squirmed and fought to stay within its folds, but then finally, he fell from the cloak and landed in a heap on the floor.

"No, you mustn't," he whispered. His once booming voice had suddenly become a weak, squeaky whine. Only moments ago the master of the beasts had seemed strong and fearful even to the monsters, but there on the floor, no longer guarded by the shroud, the figure didn't look frightening or threatening; in fact, he appeared almost comical and just a little bit pathetic. He was a snively little man with a weak, narrow jaw, stringy black hair, a pencil mustache, and long sideburns, wearing a bright, polka-dot costume covered by a tall, colorful top hat.

"No...no..." the beastmaster protested weakly. But Spike paid no attention. He continued pulling until he dragged his prey completely out from beneath the cloak. After the beastmaster's figure emerged, the cloak finally wilted, and collapsed to the floor. Spike then stopped dragging his master forward, and turned to face him. The monster let out a piercing roar.

"Oh boy..." I whispered. "This is going to get ugly."

And sure enough, Spike pounced, and landed right on the beastmaster's chest. His terrible fangs and claws began shredding clothes and flesh like a buzz saw cutting through a birthday cake. Spike lifted his head for a moment and roared, and in a flash the other monsters joined him, tearing their master to pieces. As Dunk and I watched in horror, bits of the beastmaster's costume, hat, and well...*him*, came flying through the air at us. In moments, it was over. The monsters stepped back, and the beastmaster staggered toward us. The weight of the beasts' vicious stares fell upon us as the beastmaster handed Dunk the whip, whose limp form he had dragged along with him. Once Dunk grasped it, the whip immediately sprung back to life, arising and waving like a flag in the wind.

"Now it's your turn!" the beastmaster's half-eaten lips gurgled, and then he melted into a gooey mess on the floor.

"OK, I am *not* cleaning this up," I muttered. Meanwhile, the monsters now rounded on us and began circling.

"Here, take this!" Dunk cried, trying to hand off the whip to me. "I don't want it!"

"No, Dunk!" I cried. "That whip was handed to you for a reason. You have to face this for yourself!"

Even as I spoke the words, the lion roared, and then glowered at Dunk, eyeing him like a nice, juicy rib steak.

"Oh, mama..." Dunk whimpered, pulling the whip back defensively. Right then, the whip once again came to life, arising and squirming about like a snake.

And then it *was* a snake – the end of the whip sprouted a serpent head that hissed and snapped in every direction. It lashed out at the beasts, making them fall back, but then turned and, spotting me, reared itself into a coil.

"N-nice snake," I said gently. "Good snake...Um, Polly want a cracker?"

Yes, I know that was lame. I don't know why I said that – it just somehow spilled out of my mouth. The snake hissed, and then lunged at me, snapping its jaws inches from my face.

"Remember," I whispered to myself. "It just wants to scare me. This monster won't do me any real harm..."

It was just as I was speaking those words that the snake lunged forward again, and its fangs bit deep into my flesh. I screamed.

Now when you are standing with a monster-snake thrashing about while its fangs are sunk into your arm, all bets are off. You'll do pretty much anything to get loose, and that includes swinging your arm wildly, smacking the head of the snake with anything you can get your hands on, and cussing with words that would get you a gazillion detentions if they were ever heard in school. Finally, one wild swing of my arm sent the head of the snake flying across the room. But it clearly wasn't done with me, as it coiled itself back up and quickly slithered in my direction. It hissed, and lunged at me again.

"Hey!" I shouted as I threw myself to the floor, banging my already bruised chin once more. "Ooowwww! Dunk!

Keep that thing away from me!"

"What do you want *me* to do?" Dunk shouted.

"Hello, you *are* holding its tail, aren't you? So, control it!" I roared. "That thing is in your hands for a reason! Use it! Use it to fight the monsters!"

"How?"

"Oh, come on!" I cried. "It's a whip! Use it like one!"

The snake lunged at me again. Fortunately I was able to jump aside, which threw me clear of the snake's fangs. Unfortunately, those fangs turned out to be the least of my problems. A low, rumbling growl broke out all around me. I lifted my light, and saw that I was now completely surrounded by horrible beasts that were licking their lips as if I'd make a rather tasty appetizer.

"Um, Dunk," I called out. "Anytime now would be good..." But the room remained silent except for the growling of the monsters closing in on me. I was trying not to panic, but there was no way to escape, and when I pointed my light at the monsters it had no effect. The lion came in close and roared, opening his jaws so wide that I could see his tonsils. He tensed to strike.

Just then, a loud snapping sound filled the air. The monsters turned and roared, but then the sound shot out again, and they slowly backed off. Another snap, and the monsters roared again, but then began circling, marching like trained beasts at the circus. I looked over at Dunk, and he was rearing and flinging the whip at the beasts. Wherever Dunk pointed it, the whip cracked, and the biting serpent head drove the monsters back.

"You're doing it Dunk!" I shouted. "You're taking control!"

"Yeah!" he shouted back. "But now what?"

At just that moment, the spike-eared monster broke formation, and dashed straight at Dunk. Before he could react, the beast grabbed the whip in its teeth and tried to pull

it from his grasp.

"Don't let go, Dunk!" I shouted. "Don't give up control of the..."

But even as I spoke, Spike wrestled the whip from Dunk's hand, and then held it aloft in his gristly paw. Dunk scurried back next to me as Spike cracked the whip and let out a triumphant, squeaky roar. The other beasts roared in approval.

"Now what?" Dunk asked.

"You have to go take it back!" I said as I pointed my light at the monsters. "You have to take back control and show these monsters that you're not afraid of them!"

"I am not afraid of them," a voice called out.

"Right, that's what I said..."

But I stopped, because I suddenly realized that it wasn't Dunk's voice that had spoken. I looked over at him, but he simply shrugged.

"I am not afraid of them," the voice called out again. Dunk and I both followed the sound of the voice, which seemed to be coming from the floor near where the collapsed shroud had landed. I shined the light from my RevealeR there, and on the ground, sticking out from beneath the fallen cloak, was the grotesque, frozen face of the clown mask. Only now, that face was moving.

"I have no fear, for I am the true master of the beasts," the mask droned.

Meanwhile, Spike cracked the whip, and the monsters growled, and began circling us.

"That monster is in control of the beasts now," I said. "And I don't think he's telling them to fetch us some peanuts and Cracker Jack."

"What should I do?" Dunk asked again.

"You've got to get that whip back from Spike!"

"You mean that *jackal?*"

"Whatever! You can call him Bugs Bunny for all I care! Just get the whip!"

Right then, an alarm went off in the back of my head, like some important clue had just slipped out, but I was too focused on trying to avoid being on the monsters' dinner menu to notice.

"Use *me*," the mask called out again. Dunk looked up at me, and then back at the talking mask.

Then the whip cracked once more.

You know how sometimes things happen so quickly that you can't even react to them, but other times everything seems to slow down, so that you feel like you could just run around and catch every raindrop before it falls? Well this was like both at the same time. Dunk dove forward just as the beasts stopped circling and attacked. They leapt and clawed at him as he rushed ahead. I could see it all like it was happening in slow-motion, but I seemed to be moving even slower, like I was swimming through molasses.

"Stop! Get back!" I cried, but my words seemed weightless, floating away without ever reaching their target. Meanwhile, Dunk plowed right through the mass of monsters and dove to the floor.

"Forget the whip," the mask echoed. "Only I can save you."

Dunk crawled across the floor from where he had landed and grabbed the mask. He stood and held it up triumphantly.

"No, Dunk!" I called out. "You need to...NO! LOOK OUT!"

But it was too late. Spike cracked the whip, and the lion-monster grabbed Dunk's leg and hoisted him up like a side of beef. Dunk dropped the mask, and his eyes grew wide with terror as the beast's eyes fixed on his.

"NO!" I cried.

But at that very moment, the beast sunk its fangs into Dunk's leg.

"AAAAIIIIEEEE," Dunk howled in pain and fear. He kicked at the monster with his free leg, and the monster's jaws came loose.

"No!" I shouted. "This is wrong! This isn't supposed to happen!"

And as I spoke, the bubbles of light from my RevealeR grew sparse and faded. I ran forward to help fight off the attack, but the other monsters cut me off. Meanwhile, as Dunk kept kicking at the monster's head, his dangling arm swung across the floor, and he clutched blindly for anything to use as a weapon. But there was nothing for him grab onto, until his extended fingers brushed up against something lying on the ground.

"The...the mask!" he shouted as he strained to reach further.

"Use me," the mask repeated. "Only I can save you."

"If only I can reach it..."

Right then, the monster opened its jaws to bite again, and Dunk's kick landed square on its teeth. The monster howled in pain, and Dunk fell to the floor. The lion quickly recovered and tried to bite at him, but Dunk rolled to where the mask lay and picked it up. Without another word, he thrust the clown-mask onto his face. Only nothing happened.

"That's no good, Dunk!" I shouted angrily. "We need the whip!" My RevealeR grew hot in my hand, and some of the light bubbles cascading out of it turned reddish, and grew weaker by the moment.

So, no need to tell you that with Dunk standing there with his face looking like a clown, the two of us surrounded by monsters that were slowly closing in on us, and my light fading fast, things weren't looking too good.

"Oh, could this get any worse?" I grumbled.

Of course it could.

"Grrrrrr…" came a low snarl from right behind me.

Chapter Fifteen – The True Mask

I ducked, just as the spike-eared monster's jaws took a bite out of the air where my head had just been. I dove over by Dunk and pointed what little light I could muster at the monsters encircling us.

"NO!" Dunk shouted through the mask. "Stay back!"

But the beasts kept advancing.

"You should have listened to me!" I said angrily. "You should have gone for the whip!"

"Stay **back**!" he shouted again. But this time, something was different.

"Dunk," I said. "Your voice…it's changed."

"**Stop**!" He commanded, his voice deeper, raspier.

The beasts, who had been slowly closing in on us, hesitated.

"**Get back**!" Dunk shouted. His voice was now a low, beastly growl. The beasts snarled, but held back.

"I…I don't understand," I muttered. "What's happening?" And with those words, the light bubbles from my RevealeR began to flicker. I swung the dying beam around the room, and reached back to grab Dunk by the arm.

"I don't know what's going on, but stay close," I whispered, "We need to stick together."

But when I grasped for his arm, my hand filled with fur. My whole body cringed, like it does when Janine stomps on my foot with her steel-toed boots.

"Um, Dunk?" I called out weakly, spinning around to peer into the inky air. I quickly turned the RevealeR back upon the figure behind me, and in its weak, sputtering flashes I saw the shape of the one whose arm I was grasping. It was a huge, hunched, hairy-looking form with floppy ears hanging from the sides of its pear-shaped head.

"Dunk?" But the figure simply howled in response.

"I knew it!" I hissed, pulling away from him and falling deeper into the darkness. "I *knew* you were just like them!"

I spun in every direction, pointing my nearly useless RevealeR into the blackness that drew tight around me like a noose. The beam flashed on and off again and again, with sporadic sputters of bubbles erupting out. Alone in the dark, I braced myself as hungry growls surrounded me completely.

"They don't eat you," I whispered to myself. "They don't eat you. They just want to scare you..."

At that very moment another loud lion's roar pierced the

darkness. Against my will, my knees began shaking.

"They just want to scare you....and they're pretty darn good at it!"

Just then, sharp claws slashed silently through the air and raked my coat. In one of the brief flashes of light, I looked down at the shreds of my sleeve and saw bloody gashes on my arm. I was stunned, but before I could react, the monsters were upon me, grabbing and tearing at my coat. Two of the monsters grabbed my arms, and then out of the darkness came Spike, his black eyes fixed on me in an evil leer.

"No," I whispered. "No, this can't be happening..." But Spike came in close, rose above me, and poised his claws to strike.

"**Get back!**" a beastly growl shouted. Spike looked up and snarled, but whatever was behind me roared in return. Spike hissed, but backed off, and the other monsters dropped their grip on me.

"Wow, it looks like I've been..." but the word 'saved' died in my throat as Dunk stepped forward into the weak sputters still pulsing from my RevealeR. But it wasn't Dunk, it was...I don't know, a sort of cross between Dunk and some kind of huge animal. A Dunk-monster. He had long, shaggy auburn hair all over, fat, bushy fingers with long claws on the end, and a bulldog face with a short snout, fangs, and droopy cheeks. Even as I watched, the features of his face continued morphing: the nose turned black, the nostrils became slits, the snout pushed out like an accordion, and the fangs lengthened. It was just like watching a werewolf movie, except in this case, the wolf was more like a shaggy sheepdog whose tongue hung out and dripped slobber all over me.

"Euwww!" I cried, pushing him away with unexpected ease. "Get off me, you...you *dog*!"

The Dunk-monster growled at me, but then looked around to see the other monsters closing in on us. He roared, and the monsters all fell back, even Spike, although he kept giving Dunk a nasty, sideways glower. Dunk roared again, and then the monsters did something really shocking. They *bowed.* They bowed to the Dunk-monster like he was a king or something. And then, even more surprisingly, they spoke.

"You are the one," growled the harsh voice of the lion.

"Lead us," hissed the T-rex.

"We obey," said Spike, although there was clear resentment in his squeaky voice.

"You are the one," roared the tiger.

"I knew it!" I shouted. "I knew the monsters were talking to you! But why? How are those words scary?"

But the Dunk-monster turned and glared at me. Well, actually, *not* at me. He growled in my direction, and a squeaky snarl answered back. I looked up, and instantly hit the ground. Spike had snuck behind me and his sharp fangs were about to chow down on my head. In an instant, Dunk jumped onto Spike, and they clawed and bit at each other ferociously. The battle didn't last long: Spike quickly backed down and cowered, but his eyes still followed me hungrily. Dunk roared, and Spike hissed in return, but retreated.

"Thanks," I said as I stood and backed my way toward Dunk. "I guess that mask was a good idea after all."

But as I stepped closer, Dunk's hairy paws grabbed me.

"**Rex, TJ, hold him,**" Monster-Dunk barked as he shoved me over to the T-rex and the tiger monsters. They grabbed my arms and held them at my side. At that moment, I realized that Dunk was not protecting me.

I was his prey.

So there I was, alone and helpless against a roomful of monsters. Now I don't mind telling you, it was a terrifying situation to be in even for a fearless monster detective, but strangely, it felt somehow familiar. I looked around at the monsters, and somehow they seemed to be coming into clearer focus.

"Rex, the T-rex," I whispered, and my head then swung around. "TJ, the tiger, and Spike..."

But then I remembered that Dunk had called him by a different name.

"No, not Spike...the *Jackal!*" I sniffed the air, which was filled with the scent of spoiled cheese and old socks, and realization struck me like a hammer. My RevealeR, held tight in the hand pinned at my side, suddenly burst with strong, steady white light. The monsters howled and covered their eyes at the sudden brightness, but they held tight to my arms and the RevealeR's beam remained stuck pointing uselessly at the floor.

"I get it!" I said. "I understand now, Dunk!" But Dunk, or whatever it was that he had become, answered back, "**You don't know anything! You don't know what it takes to be me! You don't know what I have to do to lead them!**" And then he came in close, and slapped the RevealeR from my hand. It hit the floor with a thud, and its beam reflected across the floorboards, giving the room a faint, eerie glow. Surrounded, alone, and defenseless, I felt Dunk's huge, canine fangs brush against my cheek. His hot breath stung my throat.

"I know you don't have to do *this*, Dunk," I pleaded as I struggled against the creatures that held me. "You don't have to be the same as them to control them. You don't have to be a monster!"

"**Why should I listen to you?**" His voice was a harsh, raspy bark. "**You don't care. You hate me.**" I looked up at him, and stared through that horrible, beast-like mask deep into his eyes. They were as blue as the ocean just like Jeannine had said. I stopped squirming. She had seen something in those eyes, something more than a football player or a bully. Now I needed to do the same.

"It...it's true that I never liked you," I admitted. "You've been nothing but mean to me. But I came here to help you just the same. I came and fought beside you, fought your monsters and bled with you! And I did it because... because I know you can be better than this!"

Dunk hesitated, and his head began to twitch. I leaned forward right into his face.

"I know what side I'm on here, Dunk," I said. "Do you?"

Dunk shook and darted like there was a bee circling his head. The monsters holding me looked on curiously, except for Spike, who growled, and circled impatiently. Dunk crouched, and put his hands to his head.

"This doesn't have to be you, Dunk," I said softly. "You can be more."

Dunk looked up at me, his blue eyes pained, but clear. I held my breath.

"**No**," he finally said. I gasped, and the monsters snickered wickedly.

"**No**," Dunk repeated. "**This is *not* me**." And then he grabbed tightly the sides of the mask and pulled hard. It stretched a bit, but remained stuck to his face. Dunk pulled again, even harder, and cried out in pain. He doubled over as he strained and struggled to tear the mask off, but it clung to his face like it was held on by Krazy Glue.

"**Noooo**," Dunk cried. "**Get...off...**" And as he kept pulling, the mask began to rise, but seemed to be taking a big portion of Dunk's face along with it. His whole head stretched like taffy as the mask lifted inch by inch from his face. Through horribly stretched out lips, he fought to speak.

"**You...will not...tell me...WHO I AM!**"

And then, just like that, the mask popped off. Dunk stared at it a moment, then looked up at me. He nodded. But right then, the monsters all began to howl. The two holding me dropped their grip and then dashed and jumped around in a frenzy. Dunk crawled over to me, and then suddenly...

Snap! The sound of the whip caught everyone's attention. We all looked up, and there was Spike, the Jackal-monster, holding up the whip. His evil eyes shone gleefully as he cracked the whip again and again, making the monsters fall into place behind him. Then he turned his malevolent glare on me and Dunk.

"It's him," Dunk said as he helplessly watched the Jackal approach. "I see it now. He's the one. He's my true monster."

"I know."

Dunk looked back at me apologetically.

"I should have gone for the whip," he said. "You were right all along." I stared at him.

"No, I wasn't. I was wrong. About a lot of things," I admitted. "But I'm not wrong anymore."

And then I stood and faced the oncoming monsters straightaway.

"Wait! What are you doing?!" Dunk shouted while the Jackal licked his lips as he crept toward me. I held my ground. The Jackal growled something back at the other monsters, who dropped back, and then he turned to me and coiled up like a spring. I knew he was about to pounce.

"Wait for it..." I whispered to myself. "One more second..."

The Jackal jumped at me, raking his claws at my face, but at the same moment I dove past him to where my RevealeR lay on the ground. I grabbed it, and it grew warm in my hand as I spun to face the Jackal once more. He turned and prepared to strike again. Those horrid jaws bared their fangs while a low, menacing growl escaped from his deformed, drooling lips. His body tensed again, crouching in preparation for another attack.

"Look out!" Dunk yelled. "He's going to pounce again! I can't stop him!!"

I just glared right back at the monster, not moving an inch.

"I told you before," I whispered fiercely, "I'm not afraid of you."

And I shined my RevealeR at the monster, and that hideous beast froze, and began to shake. He roared angrily, but I stepped in close and pointed the light right up at the monster's face, and the sound changed to a howl of pain. And then he began to shrink.

"Yessss!" I hissed triumphantly. The transformation continued: the monster's fangs retreated back into his jaw, and the tangled fur on his head grew into a longer, shaggy brown mane. The snout melted, and the eyes, though they remained wild and brutal, took on a decidedly human shape. As human as the rest of that ugly puss, anyway.

"It...it's..." Dunk stuttered.

"Hey Dunk," the monster hissed in a sour, oily voice. "What are you doing hanging out with a freakin' little wimp like this?"

"It's...*Jacko!*" Dunk finally roared.

"That's right, Dunk," I said flatly. "It's Jacko. This is the face of your true monster."

"But...but how? Why?" Dunk stuttered as he stumbled back into a seated position on the floor.

"You already know," I insisted. "The truth is right in front of you. You just have to choose to see it."

Dunk breathed in short gasps, and looked down, unwilling to meet the gaze of his beast. Meanwhile, the other monsters seemed confused and lost. They began roaring, baying, snarling...you name it, as though crying out for someone or something to give them direction.

"See the truth, Dunk," I said. "See the truth about them all." And I turned the beam of the RevealeR on the other monsters. Bathed in its clear, powerful light, they melted, and their bestial forms morphed before our eyes – fangs became facemasks, claws became taped fingers, and striped fur became numbered uniforms.

"My team..." Dunk whispered.

The beastly roars became loud, cheering voices as the monsters completed their transformation. There surrounding us were Dunk's true monsters: his teammates. His friends. I looked around the room, and through the hazy darkness I saw that our battleground had changed as well. The bars of the cage melted into the floor to become yard markers, and the distant circus stands turned into field goal uprights and stadium seats. Strangely though, the faint sound of circus music and the hum of cheering crowds were unchanged. Meanwhile, the monsters let out screeching war whoops and banged their huge, helmeted heads together like rams. Then they turned and began circling around us.

"So Dunk," TJ called out. "What should we do?"

"Show us the way," said Rex.

"Make us winners, Dunk."

"C'mon, Dunk. You *are* the team captain," the oily voice of Jacko McNulty said viciously. "You're the one who gets it done, right?"

"I...I don't... I don't know what to do..." Dunk stuttered, looking at me for guidance. "You said I didn't need the mask! So tell me what to say to them! Tell me how to control them without it!"

"I can't, Dunk," I said. "You already know what you have to do. But no one can do it for you."

Dunk's glance turned angry for a moment, but then his eyes fled once more. Just then, the largest of the monsters put its hands to its head and lifted off the helmet. It was Truck.

"Don't worry, Dunk," the monster said. "We're all behind you." Dunk glared at him.

"Really, Truck?" Dunk hissed. "You got my back?"

"I got your back, Dunk," Truck replied.

"Funny," Dunk snarled. "It didn't seem that way when you were jumping through hoops for Jacko. It didn't seem that way when you were taking a piece out of my leg."

"Whatsamatter, *pretty boy*?" Jacko roared gleefully. "Can't take it? Like we didn't already know that!"

"Don't talk like that," Truck said. "Dunkaroo is gonna lead us to victory. You're gonna bring it home for us, aren't you, buddy?"

And then Truck glared at Dunk. His eyes were fiery orbs.

"Aren't you?" the monster's voice echoed menacingly.

Dunk shivered, and the circle of monster football players (and really, is there any other kind?) growled, and began to tighten around him.

"Aren't you?" they all echoed.

"Trapped..." he muttered as he cowered in the face of the monsters. Before they could seal him in, I stepped up shined the RevealeR right in their eyes. The monsters howled and staggered back as I pointed the light at one face after another. Each recoiled from the stark brightness, but there were too many of them, and I had to keep shifting from one to the other to keep them at bay.

"That won't hold them back for long," I warned. "The only way to finish this is for you to confront them!"

"Can't do it..." he mumbled, trembling. "I can't face them without the mask."

"You can do it," I assured. "You're the one who gets it done!"

"I'm *not!*" he wailed. "I'm not some magician who can make miracles happen! I've just been lucky, OK?" Then Duncan Williams, the big, tough, bullying jock, met my gaze. His eyes were full of tears.

"After every win, those guys all pat me on the back and say, '*You did it again, Dunk! You're the one who gets it done!*' But there's always been someone else who stepped up with a great run, a great block, or a great catch that made me look good, even when I messed up! Like that championship-winning touchdown I told you about? I was throwing it to Rexie, but it was deflected! It was pure luck that it ended up in Jacko's hands!"

Dunk put his head in his hands.

"I'm just a fake," he moaned. "And once those guys see that, I'm toast."

His anguish was like chocolate pudding to the monsters, who grew larger and stronger. Their forms hardened, and grew into dark, lumbering gargoyles with thick stone limbs and spiked battle armor. They began to close in on us again in spite of the bright light from my RevealeR.

"Um," I mumbled. "We've got a problem here..."

Just then, another voice cried out, "I've got it covered!" Dunk and I both followed the sound of the voice. There on the floor lay the mask where Dunk had dropped it. Its features were now those of the big dog-monster Dunk had been, and its voice was the dog's harsh, raspy bark.

"Just put the ball in my hands," the mask boasted. "I'm the one who gets it done!" Dunk went to grab the mask, but just then the advancing team of monsters, now big as houses, raised their stone arms and struck at us.

"Move!" Dunk shouted, shoving me aside just as stone fists crashed into the floor where I was crouched. Dunk dove and rolled across the floor, landing right next to the mask, which still lay where he had dropped it.

"Only I can save you," the mask called to him. Dunk reached down and picked it up.

"That's it," the mask said. "Put me on. Only I am strong enough to control them."

Dunk brought the mask to his face, but then hesitated. He looked over at me.

"It's the only way," he whispered, but I shook my head.

"You don't have to be that person, Dunk," I called out as I dove out of the path of another of the stone beasts. "You don't need the mask. You can control your monsters without it."

But even as I spoke, the monsters drew in closer.

"Don't you get it?" Dunk shouted, spinning back to me, "Everyone counts on me! I can't be weak. I have to be a winner!"

"You *are* a winner! With the game on the line, you've come through time and time again."

"But I'm afraid every time," Dunk confessed. "Afraid I'm going to mess it all up. Afraid everyone will stop looking at me like they do. Like I'm a hero. If I make just one wrong move, it will all fall apart."

Dunk's eyes, those ocean-deep blue eyes, fixed on me, and in that brief instant, I fell inside them. For a moment, I looked out on the world through his eyes, and felt his pain and fear as if they were my own. I blinked, and I was myself again, only I suddenly saw Duncan Williams - *really* saw him - for the first time.

"I...I understand," I whispered, even as the monsters closed in around us.

"Look out!" Dunk shouted as the huge stone figures rose to strike. "Duck and cover!"

"No, Dunk," I said calmly. "Stop ducking."

"Are you crazy?!" he cried out as he dove and rolled, still clutching tightly to the mask. "We'll be splattered all over the floor!"

"It's time, Dunk," I announced. "It's time to choose."

"Choose? What are you talking about?"

"It's either you, or the mask, Dunk. You have to decide whether to be the person you hope to be, or the one you think everyone else expects of you."

"But I don't know which one I really am!" Dunk protested.

"A very wise person told me that we don't *know* who we are, we *choose*. Decide who you are going to be, Dunk. You can't let fear or anything else get in your way."

Dunk looked at the monsters and then down at the mask. His moment of truth was upon him, and we both knew it. He hesitated, but then took a deep breath, straightened up – and dropped the mask. The monsters snickered and drew in close around him. The largest one – Truck, raised his stony fist, and Dunk shook and grimaced as it swung down at him.

"Gee," I whispered to myself. "I hope I'm not wrong about this."

The monster's fist struck Dunk, and the entire room shook like an earthquake. Dunk squinted, but then gradually opened his eyes. He checked himself out, and an expression of shock and disbelief washed over his face when he found himself intact. He looked around at the monsters, who pounded the ground, making the room shake. But in spite of the tremors, Dunk grew steadier, and began to stand firmer, straighter.

"I...I don't get it," he stuttered. "Those things are made of stone. I thought I'd be a pile of goo by now."

"They *look* like stone to you," I explained. "Because they're all wearing masks too."

"The monsters?"

"Your teammates. Don't you remember what you told me about why they all follow you?"

"Because they think I make them win."

"You think so? And do you win *every* game? No, they

follow you because, win or lose, they can count on you to stand in there and take the heat for them. You give it your all, no matter how grim things look, no matter how much you hurt. You show them the guy they want to be."

"But I'm always afraid!"

"Dunk, you think all those other guys don't feel afraid too?" I asked. "Look again. See the truth about them, and then maybe you can finally face the truth about yourself."

And I pointed my RevealeR at the stone football players, and its light finally did what it was supposed to do. They shrank, shriveling until they were no more than the normal size and shape of Dunk's teammates, who, even without uniforms and armor, were still pretty big and ugly, now that I think about it.

"Look at them, Dunk," I instructed. "See the *whole* truth this time."

"Tell us," the football team said as one. "Someone must tell us what to do." Truck, Rex, and the others looked to Dunk as though expecting something, but Jacko backed out of the circle, and raised his arm.

He still held the whip. The others faced him and then fell back and bowed, but Dunk stood firm. Jacko raised the whip high over his head. Only now it wasn't a whip anymore. The cord reeled in, and the object melted and changed, growing smaller, tighter, and cylindrical, with white laces lining one side. Big evil eyes popped up along the top, just above the laces.

"A football," I realized. "The monster really *was* a football after all."

"It's mine!" Jacko shouted. "I'm in charge here! This ball is…"

Suddenly, the laces of the football parted, and pus spewed out as huge, dagger-like fangs grew in the space between the stitches. Before anyone could move, the newly-formed jaws opened wide, and then chomped down on Jacko's arm. The Jacko-monster screamed as the demonic football gobbled up his hand and chewed and tore at his wrist and forearm, which began spewing green slime from the bite wounds.

"No, get off!" Jacko cried as he struggled with his other hand to pull the football from his arm. He finally tore it loose and struggled to hold its jaws closed, but it squirmed and fought itself free, and he began fumbling with it like a hot potato.

"Help me!" Jacko pleaded as he sank to his knees. "Somebody take this thing!" He tried to hand the monster over to Truck, but the big, hulking brute backed away. Jacko turned to his teammates, but they all hid behind Truck, pressing in so tightly that they melted together. Desperately, Jacko turned to Dunk and held out the squirming, man-eating football, while the football team monsters gazed on with an expectant look on all of their faces.

"It's up to you now, Dunk. You're gonna take over for us, aren't you, buddy?" Truck growled as his teammates' heads weaved around his face. His voice, though it was still deep and stony, faltered.

I pointed the light from my RevealeR right at Truck's eyes, which were wide and glassy.

"Can you see it now?" I asked. "Can you see it in their faces?" Dunk squinted, and stared, but then his head slowly, knowingly nodded.

"Yes, I see it now," Dunk said without taking his eyes off the monsters. "You...you all need me to take the ball, don't you? You need me to take it because you're afraid to do it yourselves. You're so afraid you'll get blamed for losing that you want the ball to be in someone else's hands. *My* hands."

"You...you're gonna bring it home for us, aren't you, buddy?" Truck pleaded. "Aren't you?"

"Aren't you?" echoed Rex and the others. The words echoed again and again; not a demand, but rather a cry for help.

Duncan Williams stepped up to the Truck-monster and stared it in the face. The beast had shrunk down to life sized, which for Truck was still huge, but Dunk moved in close, until they were nose to chin.

"Yes, Truck," Dunk said, his eyes never wavering from the monster's face. "Yes, I'm gonna bring it home."

"No!" cried a raspy, bestial voice. Dunk's eyes followed the voice down to the floor, where the mask still lay. Only it wasn't lying anymore. The mask arose, and stood on its chin. Its face and its voice were now hollow, distorted versions of Dunk's own. "No, you can't!" it bellowed. "You cannot win without me!"

Dunk stood firm. He stared that hideously deformed version of his own face right in the eyes.

"You don't scare me anymore," Dunk said.

Dunk's words struck the surface of the mask like a blow. It rippled like a windswept pond, and whined a deep, ghostly moan. The face melted, and its features bent and morphed until a new visage emerged: Jacko.

"You ain't no leader," the Jacko-mask cackled. "You're a perfumed, prissy little momma's boy. You're weak."

"No, *you* are the weak one," Dunk replied. "I can see that now."

And then the mask melted again, and reformed into the face of a craggy middle-aged man wearing a football team cap on his head and a whistle around his neck. Dunk's football coach, Mr. Jenner.

"You're no football player," the coach-mask said. "You're soft and slow, and you just don't have what it takes."

Dunk froze, but then glared harshly.

"I know who I am. And I *AM* a football player, like my father before me."

And with that, he reached over and pulled the football from the Jacko-monster's grasp. Dunk clutched it securely, but the monster football's jaws stretched out from under Dunk's arm all the way up to his head, and its huge fangs sprang forth and opened wide. I shined the RevealeR at it, but it had no effect, and the jaws that had chewed off his teammate's arm prepared to take a bite out of Dunk's head.

"Dunk, look out!" I cried out. "Something's gone wrong! The RevealeR isn't working!"

But Dunk just stood there holding tight to the football monster as its jaws snapped shut.

"Go ahead, take your best shot," he said to the ball as his face disappeared into the monster's mouth and its teeth dug into his head. The football-monster chomped and chewed happily, and then I shuddered as its gaze turned toward me. It smiled broadly, eyeing me like it was just finishing the main course and I was the dessert. But just then, the slimy, lace-stitched mouth grimaced, and shook. Its teeth, though wrapped around Dunk's face, stretched like rubber, and Dunk's head squeezed back out. The monster struggled to keep its jaws locked around Dunk's face, but they bent and slipped off like he was a greased pig. Maybe it was all that hair gel.

"I told you," Dunk said firmly, appearing none the worse for wear. "I'm not afraid of you anymore."

The football quivered, and then with a final mad wail, it exploded with light. Caught in the blinding radiance, the mask and all of the other monsters howled, and then began shaking. Their forms melted together into a single shuddering mass, which roared and crumpled as it shrank, until finally the entire heap collapsed to the floor, empty. Dunk and I stood there a moment, staring at it as it lay there, still and toothless. I pulled out my MonsterScope and checked it out. The scope was clear at last, showing that the cloth had lost all of its power. Still clutched tightly in Dunk's grip was the football, which was now just a ball – the energy that had given it life was gone.

"There it is, Dunk," I said. "There's your horrible monster. Now that you've faced the truth about it, all that's left for you to do is pick it up."

Dunk slowly reached down and lifted the flattened bundle. The remains of the shrouded monsters had come together to form a navy-colored mesh shirt with a big number 11 on the back and the word ASHFORD across the chest in large block letters.

"Your uniform?" I asked.

Dunk nodded.

"My captain's jersey," he said, pointing to the bold letter 'C' stitched into the upper left shoulder of the shirt. "But why would my shirt be a monster?"

"It's what marks you as the team leader," I said. "It's what sets you apart."

Dunk looked up at me. Again, he nodded.

"Yeah, I guess," he said. He looked down at the football in his hand, and raised it to his face. "But I think I can handle it now. Win or lose, I'm ready to be the one. I'm ready to do what I need to do."

"You know what?" I said thoughtfully. "So am I."

Dunk snickered.

"Yeah, well...you've got guts, kid," he chuckled. "But I don't think you'll make the cut. Maybe when you grow a little."

"I'm not talking about *football*," I hissed. "I'm talking about learning to see with someone else's eyes, like my mentor, Bigelow Hawkins told me. I'm ready to do what it takes to be a true detective."

"That helps you fight monsters?"

"It does. It's like I told you. We need to understand the monsters in order to fight them. Even with my MonsterScope and RevealeR, I had trouble seeing your monsters until I tried to see things the way you see them."

Dunk's head nodded slowly.

"You needed to think like a football player. Getting into the head of your opponent and guessing his strategy and weaknesses."

I nodded back. "I guess your way of looking at things isn't so different from mine after all. We're both trying to learn how to be more than we thought we could be."

Dunk's eye twitched, and he looked away. His head jerked a bit, but then he looked again at the still, lifeless football. Dunk lifted it high over his head and pumped a few fake throws at the wall, but then turned his hand over and tossed the ball lightly into his closet.

"What are you doing?" I asked.

"Just cleaning up," Dunk answered. "My dad freaks out

if my room gets to be a mess."

I laughed.

"You got a problem with that?" Dunk growled. I quickly bit my lip.

"No, but don't you think that your room is the least of your worries?"

"What are you talking about?"

"Well, *you're* kind of a mess," I pointed out. "Won't your dad freak out when he sees all those cuts and bruises?"

Dunk shrugged.

"My dad was a football player, like me," he answered. "He'll say just clean it, wrap it, and get back on the field."

"Wow. I wish my parents would be so easy. If my mom knew what I was doing, she'd probably lock me in my room. You know how moms can be."

Dunk didn't answer. Instead, he knelt beside his bed and picked up something from the floor. It was the picture of his mother. In our battle with the monsters, the frame had been smashed, and the glass had broken. Dunk brushed the shards from the image, which was now tattered and torn. He continued facing away and held his jersey to the side of his face. For the longest time, neither one of us spoke.

"Look, if you're not going to help me clean up," he finally said, "then why don't you just clear out of here."

"Now is that any way to talk to the person who just helped you conquer your deepest, darkest fears?"

Oops. I might have hit a sore point there.

"You? What did *you* do?" he hissed, looking back at me sharply.

"What...What did I do?" I sputtered. "I just fought your monsters with you!"

"*You* didn't do anything," Dunk insisted. "You made *me* do all the work. I'm the one who had to defeat the monsters. You just..."

"But...but that's how it works!" I protested. "I told you

that right from the..."

"Just get out," he growled.

"Bu-but..." I stuttered.

"Just GO!"

OK, this was definitely not the boundless gratitude I was expecting from the guy I had just saved from monsters. So even though I thought I had put all of my anger at Dunk behind me, it arose again. My face bent into a scowl, and my cheeks started to burn.

"You know what?" I hissed. "Maybe Jacko was right. Maybe you're really..."

At that very moment, my RevealeR turned hot in my hands. I looked down at it, and saw dark fumes spewing out. I think that if I let it, it could have burned Dunk's room to the ground. Just then, Bigelow's words burst into my mind.

The fire that burns inside you destroys things much more precious and valuable than curtains. It wipes out judgment.

Somehow, I knew that this was the kind of moment he was talking about. I was ready – no, *eager* to say something hurtful, to do something stupid that could not be undone. Instead, I closed my eyes and brought my hands together in the way Bigelow had taught me. And it worked...a little.

"But you still haven't paid me," I hissed quietly, opening my eyes and staring at Dunk.

"Don't you worry!" Dunk shot back. "I told you before – I always pay my debts! Now get out!"

Then he turned away again, still holding the smashed photo, and clutching the jersey close to his cheek like a...

Well, I won't go there. Seeing as how I share my Teddy Bear with Bigelow Hawkins, the Great Monster Detective, I really shouldn't make fun of anything someone uses for comfort and security.

Baby blanket.

OK, I went there. Sue me.

Chapter Sixteen – Cold Comforts

So if you thought that being a heroic monster detective and helping your client overcome his dreadful monsters would lead to some *happily ever after* kind of ending…well, actually, so did I. But this whole monster detective thing is turning out to be way different than I expected. I mean, it's not like I thought there would be cheering crowds, but a little appreciation would be nice. And if Dunk's gratitude was lacking, that's nothing compared to what I faced when I got home. Mind you, I beat my curfew, no thanks to my man-eating bicycle, which broke down completely on the way and forced me to run, carrying the pieces, for nearly a mile in order to get home before the clock struck my personal witching hour. Of course, the fact that I staggered in panting and wheezing did nothing to put my parents at ease.

"What HAVE you been doing?" my mother screeched when she stormed in from the living room and saw me bent over the kitchen table propped up on one arm. As I struggled to breathe, I held up my hand as a signal to her to give me a moment to catch my breath, but somehow the message seemed lost one her.

"What happened to you?" she continued in a blistering voice. "What put you in a state like this?"

I held up my hand again, and pointed at my lungs, then tried several other gestures to try and get my message across, but my mother threw up her hands and cried out, "James! I need you in here!"

"What...what is it?" my dad called out as he came running.

Well, my dad came rushing in, not realizing that I had dropped my bicycle beside the kitchen door, so that when he banged through it, the door rebounded back and hit him square in the face.

"Ooooff!" he gasped as he was knocked back out of the room and fell to the floor. There was a long pause, which gave me a chance to regain some of my breath, and a then slight moaning sound. Finally the door squeaked as my father pressed his way slowly back into the room, holding his face gingerly with one hand. He looked down at the broken-down bicycle beside the door, and then glared up at me.

"How many times have I told you," he hissed, "not to leave your things lying..."

"Oh, never mind about that!" my mom injected loudly. "Just look at the state of him, will you! His clothes are all torn and he's covered in gashes and god knows what else!"

"These..." I stuttered. "These are the same scratches from yesterday, when I fell off my bike."

"Don't you lie to me, young man!" my mother shrieked. "Just look at that chin! Those wounds are bloody and fresh! Now tell me the truth or so help me..."

"All right, all right," I said, but even as I spoke, I could...well, *smell* her anger.

"Look, I'm sorry," I said. "I just didn't want you to worry."

"What happened!" she screeched.

"All right, all right...Ease up, Chase," my father said softly. He had taken his hand from the new bruise growing on his forehead and placed it upon her shoulder, but I think it was the fact that he called her by her name that seemed to startle her, and gave him a chance to continue. "Give the boy a chance to explain." My mom glared at him at first, but he kept his calm eyes fixed on hers, and she relented. She gave him a quick nod, and then they both turned to face me.

"Well?"

Let me tell you, a lump formed in my throat that was bigger and drier than...well, most any other big dry lump. I had no idea what to say. What could they possibly want me to tell them? I didn't want to lie, but they wouldn't believe the truth. And what lie could explain what they were seeing? Just then, I sniffed the air around me. It still carried the scent of my mother's rage, but I could also sense something behind her anger - *fear*. She was deathly afraid of what had happened to me – what *might* be happening to me. And she needed some way of making sense of it all.

"The truth is..." I finally said. "The truth is that I got into a fight. I took on some football players who were bullying me and my friends at school."

Hey, it *was* the truth, after all. I just left out the part about them all turning into horrifying beasts, slashing their claws at my head, and trying to use me as a chew toy. Sometimes when you're telling a story like that, it's best not to go into too much detail. My mother gasped, but my dad got a cold look in his eyes.

"That is it!" he shouted. "Tomorrow morning I'm coming to your school and..."

"No, Dad," I said. "No, you can't."

My mom looked at me like I had just robbed a bank, but my dad's face grew stern, but curious.

"Look, I know you and mom want to protect me. I know you want to keep me safe from anything that might ever hurt me."

"We're your parents, Will. That's what parents *do*."

"I know, Dad. But you also always say that I should learn to stand on my own two feet. Well, that's what I'm doing. There are some things I have to face for myself, and this is one of them."

"But you're just one little kid," my dad said. "You can't take on the bullies of the world."

"I can, Dad. I *have*. I can't tell you how, but I've taken care of it. They will never bother me again."

"You..." my mother stuttered. "You didn't do anything...*illegal*?"

"They won't bother you again?" my dad said. "How can you be sure?"

"Trust me," I assured. But their faces went blank. "You do trust me, don't you?"

My parents stared at me, but then their eyes turned to one another. My dad took my mother's hand in his, and they both looked down at their entwined fingers. The air was a stew of their feelings: anxiety, apprehension, pride, fear, and sadness, all surrounded and contained by an envelope of faith. They *did* believe in me. Go figure.

"Yes, Will. We trust you." My mom finally said.

She looked back up at my dad, and he nodded.

"All right, Will," he said. "I just hope you know what you're doing. But we'll leave it to you to deal with this yourself."

"Thanks, Dad...Thanks Mom," I said gratefully. My dad nodded, and my mom hesitated, but then nodded too.

Then they both turned and headed for the stairs. I sighed in relief. I watched as my dad walked up out of sight and my mom followed.

Maybe, I thought, *maybe talking to my parents isn't always such a bad idea after all.* Just then, my mom stopped halfway up the stairs and turned back to me.

"But don't think this gets you out of trouble," she said. "Go put your bicycle in the garage, and clean up the mess you made all over the floor when you dragged it into the house. And then remember to get yourself washed up before you go to bed. I don't want you leaving a pile of dirt all over my nice clean sheets." And then she continued the rest of the way up the stairs.

Well, by the time I finished cleaning everything up, I was pooped. Still, I tried calling Jeannine to tell her that everything was OK, but her mom answered the phone and told me she was in bed, and that I had no business calling so late on a school night. Needless to say, when I finally got to my room, my mind was a jumble. And there was just one person...if he actually *is* a person, that I could talk to.

"Bigelow!" I called out. "Are you here, or are you off on safari or something?"

"I'm here, Will," answered a gravelly, scratchy voice. I turned to my bed, and found him already standing beside it in his usual oversized trench coat and bowler hat. He shuffled closer, and the brim of his hat rose and fell as he checked me up and down.

"You look terrible," he said calmly. "Did everything go alright?"

"Oh, everything went fine," I answered. "The monsters were kind of rough, but me and Dunk pulled through OK."

But Bigelow kept eyeing me (not that I could actually see his eyes, but I could tell he was still looking me over).

"Perhaps you should be checked out by a doctor?" he suggested. "Some of those injuries might be more serious than they seem."

"Nah. I mean after all, it's not like the monsters would do any real harm," I said casually. Bigelow stayed silent for a moment.

"What on earth makes you say that?" he asked.

"Well, uh, I thought..." I sputtered. "Um, I mean you told me that monsters feed on fears, not people."

"That is correct," Bigelow replied.

"Well then I figured...um, that is...*Jeannine* figured that since the monsters feed off of our fears, they need to keep us alive and well. They can't feed off of us if we've been eaten, so we're not really in terrible danger."

"That's a brilliant deduction on her part," Bigelow said. "The sensible thing would be for the monsters to not actually harm you, but just keep you afraid, so that they can continue to feed off of you."

"Pretty smart, huh?" I agreed. "She really is a good detective."

Bigelow shook his head.

"She's also dead wrong," he said. "Monsters are not rational creatures, Will. Their behavior isn't always... *sensible.*"

"Are - are you saying..." I gasped. "Are you saying that I *could* get eaten alive?"

"No, not that," Bigelow snickered. "But there *is* grave danger, Will. And you must be mindful of that. You need to be cautious."

"But you taught me that I shouldn't give in to fear!"

"And so you shouldn't. But fear itself is not your enemy."

"That...that's crazy! Fear creates monsters!"

"That is true. But fear itself is not evil; in fact, it has a purpose: it keeps people safe by preventing them from doing dangerous things."

"Then..."

"Once again, it all comes down to controlling your feelings and exercising good judgment. Unrestrained fear often makes us do beastly and foolish things. It can bring out monsters in all of us. But so can recklessness."

"Or anger," he added knowingly. "You must continue to master these feelings in yourself before you can help others conquer them."

"Um, speaking of that," I said as Bigelow's words steered my thoughts in a new direction. "Lately it's been like other people's feelings have been...well, *attacking* me. It's like they float through the air and come after me."

Bigelow remained silent. I was expecting him to tell me I was imagining things, or that it was my own feelings I experienced, and I must have been confused somehow.

"That is called empathy," he finally said. "It is a sign that you are becoming a true detective."

"It is?"

"Yes, Will. Other people's feelings are always in the air, waiting to be sensed. You have only now begun to unlock your receptiveness to them. And your awareness of the feelings in the air is a very powerful and useful tool."

"This...this empathy thing. Does it ever go away?"

"It can. Do you want it to?"

"I...I don't know. It's just so confusing. At times, I didn't know if I was feeling Dunk's feelings or my own."

"Perhaps that is because they are not so different as you thought."

I winced, and looked away.

"That disturbs you?"

"No – *Yes*. Before today, it was always clear who the jerks were. But Dunk – there's more to him than just a bully. And me..."

I thought of Gerald, and how I had harshly insulted him.

"Well, lately there have been times when I... when I was a bit of a jerk too."

"Yes, the world is often more complicated than we would like. Sadly, to be a monster detective you must choose to see the world as it truly is, and in doing so, you will see many things you don't want to see."

"Then why would anyone want to *be* a detective?"

"That is a good question. After all, facing monsters is difficult, dangerous...and painful," Bigelow said. "But when we look deep into our world and ourselves and confront what we find there, we are changed. Maybe not instantly or all at once, but we grow. We become better, stronger people."

"Is that true for Dunk, too? His monsters are gone, but

how can we be sure that he has really learned his lesson?"

Bigelow shrugged.

"We can only hope," he said. My eyes lit up, and if I had been holding my RevealeR, it probably would have burned the house down.

"*Hope?*" I shouted angrily. "Hope? I fought and I suffered, and I bled, and all I have to show for it is *hope*?!!"

But Bigelow just smiled at me.

"Yes Will, hope," he said calmly. "That noblest of all human virtues. The source of your faith, and strength, and courage. It is the hope that our efforts are not in vain that enables perseverance and sacrifice. It is what makes possible all human achievement."

"Still, it doesn't seem like much of a reward for all I went through."

"True," Bigelow agreed. "But then you of all people should know that things are often more than they seem."

And with that, he hopped back on top my bed, threw the quilt over his head, and vanished.

The sun woke me again the following morning, its rays forming blazing streaks of gold and ginger that burned their way into my dreams and washed them away. My head wobbled as I blinked furiously, fighting off the call back to consciousness, but resistance failed, and so I sat up and shook my head. Try as I might, I could not remember my dreams.

"I have *got* to remember to close those shades when I go to bed," I muttered as I got up and began getting ready for school. My head was still swimming as I strode quietly down the steps and headed for the kitchen. But, though I was lost in thought, the horror of what I saw when I pushed open the kitchen door turned my blood to ice. There before my eyes were my mom and dad, wrapped around each other, arms entwined; rubbing noses and god knows what else. I covered my eyes to keep them from being burned from their sockets.

"Ahem," I coughed loudly.

My mom and dad quickly broke apart. My mother looked embarrassed, but my dad had a big smirk on his face as he sat down in his chair and picked up his morning paper.

"You- you're up early again," she mumbled awkwardly as she stepped over to the stove. Her cheeks were as red as the omelet on the skillet. "Breakfast?"

My mom lifted the pan from the stove and brought it to the table, where she slid its contents onto my plate.

"I just lost my appetite," I growled. "In fact, I may never eat again."

"Oh, don't be such a drama queen," she said impatiently. "You need nourishment. So eat up."

I can't say which made me more sick to my stomach that morning: The sight of my parents canoodling or the taste of eggs that looked and smelled like monster guts.

And hey, who would know better than me, right?

I was seriously wondering if I might puke as soon as I left the house, but as I stepped out onto the stoop, I froze in my tracks.

There, at the bottom of the steps, was a bicycle. It was old, and a bit beaten up, but it was a full ten-speed racer in electric blue with a padded seat, vinyl-wrapped handlebars, a hi-beam headlight, and all the trimmings.

"Who...?" But then I noticed a note tied to one of the handlebars. I pulled it off and read:

I always pay my debts

"Well I'll be..." I muttered. Naturally, I decided to test it out right away. I walked the bike into our garage, where I quickly adjusted the height of the seat and handlebars. I took my cable and lock off of the cracked frame of my old bike and put it on this one, and then climbed on and took off down the street.

When I glided into the school parking lot, I was smiling broadly. Of course, there was no way *that* was going to last.

"Where have you been?" Jeannine whispered fiercely as I sat down next to her in homeroom. "You weren't on the bus! Do you know how worried I've been?"

"I rode my bike," I explained. "My *new* bike...that I got as payment."

Jeannine's eyes lit up. She leaned in closer.

"So you did it?" she whispered excitedly. "Tell me! Tell me everything!"

"I sure did," I announced proudly. "Another case successfully..."

"Hilmar?" the substitute teacher called out. "Hilmar Allen?" I grimaced, but then shrugged my shoulders.

"Present," I called out, then turned back to Jeannine. "So anyway, I got there and..."

But just then, I sensed something bad coming. Maybe it was that empathy stuff Bigelow told me about. Maybe I felt the hostility in the air. Or maybe it was just the smell of spoiled cheese and old socks approaching. Anyway, I turned and ducked just as a hand shot through the air on its way toward the back of my head. I turned, and there was Jacko standing behind me. He looked startled about his blow missing me, but then that oily smile slid back across his face.

"Grew some freakin' eyes in the back of your head, Hilmar?" he cackled. "Better hope so." And then he slunk back down the aisle, with my eyes boring into him as he went.

"So?" Jeannine whispered, dragging my attention back to her. "Tell me what happened!"

"Well, I..."

But just then, the bell sounded.

"I...I'll tell you all about it at lunch. Unless you're

hanging with Timmy again?"

"And miss this story? Never!" And then she got up and marched out without another word.

Lunchtime seemed to come quickly that day, as most of my classes were surprisingly interesting. As usual, I was already in my seat waiting for Jeannine when she arrived at our lunch table.

"So," she whispered excitedly. "Tell me everything!"

"Well, I..." But just then, I spotted Gerald over by the lunch room door. He was watching us, but when he saw me looking at him, he turned and left. I sighed.

"What?" Jeannine asked.

"Gerald," I replied. "He was there by the door." I hesitated, but then added, "We really should ask him to sit with us." Jeannine's eyes widened, and I expected her to bite my head off for suggesting such a thing, but then she sighed too, and said, "I suppose we should. Do you want to go invite him? He might faint straightaway if I do it."

I nodded, and then got up and headed out to the hallway.

"Gerald," I called out as I followed him around the corner. At first he ignored me. "Gerald, wait up."

Gerald looked up at me and hissed, "What do *you* want?" He clearly wasn't going to make this easy, and I took a deep breath before answering.

"Look, I'll just come out with it. I was a jerk for saying what I did, and I'm sorry. I'll understand if you don't want to, but if you'd still like to be friends, then me and Jeannine would like to have you come sit with us at lunch."

Gerald looked suspicious.

"Jeannine will be there? She won't ditch us?"

"She'll be there. And as a peace offering, I can give you my dessert. My mom made cheesecake."

Hey, I know it was probably toxic, but there was no need to tell Gerald that. He gave me a funny look, like he was trying to smile, but his face wouldn't let him.

"Come on. I'll even let you have the seat next to Jeannine," I offered. Gerald smiled for real this time.

"You had me at cheesecake," he laughed.

"So, you forgive me?"

"Hey, that's what friends do, right?"

I smiled.

"Right," I said. We turned, but before we could take a step, our path was blocked. Gerald looked up, and froze like a deer in headlights. If only from the smell.

"Well, it's dorks on parade time, isn't it?" Jacko McNulty cackled. He stepped directly in front of me, but behind him, with his face hanging over the top of Jacko's head, was his buddy Truck. Rex and TJ flanked his sides. I looked around, but Duncan Williams was nowhere in sight.

"If it is, then you're in one of the marching bands," I barked at Jacko.

Truck snickered, and Jacko turned and glared at him.

"What? You in a marching band!" Truck chuckled. "That's funny, right?"

Jacko hissed at him, and then turned back to me.

"So, *Hilmar*," he said as he moved in closer. "Let's see if you're still talking so freakin' big when I'm done with you!"

Fire rose inside me. My cheeks began burning, and I steadied myself for battle. I didn't care if I won or lost – some part of me deep inside really, really wanted to fight. Jacko stepped up to me, but at that very moment everything took a strange and unexpected turn. Gerald...*Gerald* of all people, stepped in and cut Jacko off.

"Leave him alone!" Gerald shouted. Out of shock, Jacko straightened up (well, as straight as that twisted spine of his can get, anyway), and his eyes started blinking furiously.

"You...you talkin' to *me*?" he growled, and turned back to his teammates. "Can you freakin' believe this? Another wimpy runt thinks he can get away with mouthin' off at me!

I think we better do something about this right now, right guys?"

"I'm not afraid of you!" Gerald shouted.

Now, I'm a monster detective, but even I know the difference between being brave and stupid, and this situation had *train wreck* written all over it.

Yes, I know that I'm the one who told Gerald to show some backbone, but I didn't mean for him to show it to a bunch of animals that would rip it out for him. The fire in my veins started to rise again, but this time I bit my lip, and took a deep breath.

Just then, Duncan Williams stepped out of the bathroom door on the wall beside us, calling out, "OK guys. Let's go…" In a moment, he spotted us, and stepped in front of Jacko.

"C'mon, Jacko, let's not do this again," Dunk said. "Leave him be. He's just a little turd."

"A turd who need to be taught some manners!" Jacko growled.

"You couldn't teach a snail how to crawl," Gerald spat.

"Stay out of this, Gerald," I said. I stepped back in front of him, though I kept my eyes fixed on Jacko and Truck. "Look, I'm sorry for insulting you, OK? But we're not looking for any trouble."

Dunk gave me a curious look, but then a small smile crept across his face.

"Smart move, kid," he chuckled. "I guess you finally learned your lesson."

"*One* of us had to," I hissed. Dunk stopped chuckling. His eyes darted, but then he tapped Jacko on the shoulder.

"Come on," Dunk said, tugging him away. "We gotta eat quick and get to the gym. I've got some new drills I want to work on at recess today."

"Not now!" Jacko pulled out of his grip. "I still need to teach this little brat some…"

"Yes, now!" Dunk insisted, moving between us.

"Hey!" Jacko growled, leaning in close and pounding Dunk with a vicious glare. "Since when do you tell me what to do?"

"Since now!" Dunk shouted. "And I said lay off!" Jacko glared back at him.

"I don't freakin' listen to you, pretty boy," he growled ferociously. "You're just..."

"I'm the team captain," Dunk said fiercely. "You'll do what I tell you."

"Is that so?" Jacko hissed, as an evil grin spread across his face. "Truck! Tell Dunk the punk who's in charge around here."

Truck stepped up and stood over Dunk, but Dunk didn't back down. Instead, he turned and got right in Truck's face, staring at him eye to eye.

"Yeah, Truck," Dunk said. "Tell me who's in charge. Tell me who is going to lead us to a championship. Which of us is going to make sure that all of our hard work and training isn't going to go to waste?"

Truck blinked a bit, but then his eyes wandered like he was looking for an emergency escape on a burning plane.

"Who's the ticket, Truck? Who's the one who gets it done?"

Truck looked over at Jacko, and then back at Dunk.

"You're the ticket, Dunk," he finally said.

"So, you got my back?"

"I got your back."

Jacko's mouth started doing that fish-like opening and closing thing again.

"But...But Truck..."

"Dunk's the ticket, Jacko. He's right: we've been working all year for this. I ain't gonna let *you* throw it all away."

"But..."

"But nothing. Dunk's the ticket. End of story."

Truck then turned and loomed over Jacko, just as he had over Dunk. Unlike Dunk, however, Jacko seemed to shrink in Truck's shadow.

"Say it, *Trevor*," Dunk said firmly, glaring right into Jacko's eyes. Their stares locked on one another, and for a moment, the whole world froze. Finally, Jacko blinked, and his eyes wandered in confusion.

"All right," he said weakly. "All right, you're the ticket."

"Let's go then," Duncan Williams demanded, grabbing him and pulling him away. "We've got more important things to do than hang out in the hallway. Move it!"

"Don't think I'm done with you, squirt," Jacko called out to Gerald as Dunk dragged him off. "I...I'm gonna ...hey! Quit pulling! I...all right already!"

They were halfway down the hall before Dunk let go. Jacko turned back and shouted, "Just you stay out of my way, kid. Or you'll get what's..."

But Dunk had already turned the corner and shoved him into the next hallway.

"Whew!" I exhaled. Then I turned to Gerald and said, "Thanks, Gerald. Thanks for standing up for me." Gerald smiled.

"It feels good to be a hero, doesn't it?" he said.

"Yeah!" I said. "Come on, let's get back to the lunch room. Jeannine is waiting for us and…"

But as we turned back, our way was blocked again. I instantly braced myself for another attack, but none came. At least not the kind I expected.

There in front of us was Tiffany, the obnoxious girl from the bus, staring right at us. She was wearing her cheerleading uniform, and a look of awe that was way different than the usual sneer she gives me. In fact, with admiration painted all over her face, she looked kind of pretty. So naturally, I responded as I always do when I'm around pretty girls.

"Aba…umwa…" my mouth dribbled out. But she walked past me, and right up to Gerald.

"That was so cool, how you stood up to those bullies," she cooed.

"Hey!" I protested. "What about me?"

But neither of them seemed to hear me at all.

"You…You think so?" Gerald stuttered.

"Definitely! You were like a ferocious lion…except maybe for the hair."

"Hey!" I cried a little louder. "Am I just a piece of furniture here?"

Tiffany paused a moment, and turned to give me an inquisitive look.

"I don't know. Are you?"

I wanted to say, *"Him? I'm the one who faced those guys down!"* But my mouth simply refused to cooperate. "Aba…umwa…" is all it poured out.

"Would you," Tiffany said, turning back to speak to Gerald and waving me off like I was some irritating fly buzzing around her head, "would you like to come have lunch with me? Me and some of the girls are eating out by the bleachers, it's so nice out today."

"Would I!" Gerald said. "You bet!" He turned to go with Tiffany, but then looked back a moment and said, "Um, Will, no offense, but I think I'll pass on joining you and Jeannine today. Still friends, though, right?"

And then without even waiting for an answer, they walked off together, leaving me standing there with my mouth hanging open.

"So?" Jeannine said impatiently when I got back to the table. "Where's Gerald?"

"He, um...he got a better offer," I said, and then explained what happened in the hallway.

"Oh, those football players are so full of themselves," Jeannine said crossly after I had finished.

"I know," I agreed. "I think I liked them all better as monsters."

Jeannine blinked once or twice, and then sputtered, "Excuse me...*what*?"

So I told her the whole story – the football-monster, the hideous shroud, the wild beasts, the stone football team, everything. And give Jeannine credit: she sat hushed, eyes riveted, for the whole thing, and gasped and giggled at all the right parts.

"So go figure, the monsters were football players," she said when I had finally finished. "What a shock. They're all halfway there to begin with."

"I think maybe Gerald was right," I said. "I think they're worse in real life than they are as monsters. At least when they're monsters, we have our RevealeRs to whittle them down to size."

Jeannine looked up, and turned suddenly thoughtful.

"So, do you think that because you helped him conquer his monsters, Duncan will want to be friends with us now, just like Gerald?"

The hopeful tone in her voice was disturbing.

"No, I don't think so," I said. "He still looks at me like I'm some kind of bug he'd like nothing better than to squash."

"Well, maybe at least now, thanks to you, he'll stop picking on little kids," she said cheerfully.

"I'm not so sure," I said, shaking my head. "Dunk doesn't seem to think there's anything wrong with stuff like that. He thinks that's just the way things are."

"Well, that's easy for him to say. I mean, sure, that's the way things are for most of us," Jeannine said with her voice rising. "But it's not the way things are for *him*, is it?"

"Ah, well actually," I said. "Dunk said *he* got picked on too. He said it happens to everybody."

"Well, that's no excuse!" she answered heatedly.

I felt her sudden anger rise through the air, and paused a moment, kicking at the ground before asking my next question.

"Jeannine, did you...did *you* ever get picked on?"

"Of course! Don't you remember? In second grade, back when I was still...you know, a little bit heavy..."

"A little bit?" I whispered. She glared at me, but then went right on.

"Everyone was teasing me," she recalled. "They called me Chubby Cubbie, and lots of other mean things."

"*I* never called you any of those things."

Jeannine gave me a strange look. It was a little bit of a crooked smile, and a little bit of an appraising look.

"No, you didn't," she said, with her voice turning suddenly soft. "I remember you saw me crying when one of my so-called friends, Jaime McIntyre, started calling me that, and got right in her face and told her to stop. You were a little hero even then."

"I – I never thought of it that way," I stuttered. "I was

just standing up for you. You're my friend."

She gave me that look again.

"Yes, Will. I'm your friend."

"Erm...So, I guess maybe Dunk was right about that. Maybe it happens to everybody."

"It's still no excuse," She insisted. "Just because someone gets teased doesn't give them the right to be hurtful to someone else."

"Well then it's not just Dunk who should be nicer, is it?" I said meekly. "I suppose...I suppose we *all* have people we could treat better."

Jeannine sighed.

"I suppose so," she agreed. "Maybe everyone needs to learn their lesson now and then. But people like Duncan Williams need to learn it more!"

"Hmmm..." I said thoughtfully, as I glanced back across the room at Duncan Williams, who was sitting over at the jocks' table, laughing with his buddies. His eyes briefly caught mine, and upon seeing me watching him, his smile slipped. But at just that moment, one of his friends slapped him on the shoulder.

"Hey, Dunk," his friend said cheerfully. "You spacing or what?"

Dunk laughed, and slapped his friend back. But before he turned away, he took one last look at me. Then he returned to laughing with his gang.

"We can only hope," I muttered, turning back. "Well anyway, at least I solved the case."

"That's right!" Jeannine said, her cheerful tone having instantly returned. "Now we've both solved one case on our own, and one together. We're tied."

See, I told you she's the competitive one.

"Actually, I've solved one more case than you," I said. "The case where I fought my *own* monsters with Bigelow's help."

"Doesn't count."

"Does too."

Jeannine rolled her eyes, but then sighed.

"Fine. You're up one," she finally conceded. "So will you cheer up then?"

"Well, I still have no money, a beaten-up, second-hand bike, and except for you and maybe Gerald, no friends."

Jeannine studied me curiously.

"Well, aren't we in a 'the glass is half empty mood' today," she finally quipped. I glared at her.

"So what does the *full* half of the glass look like?"

"Let's see..." she said, "You *are* one of the smartest boys in school. You get the best grades in almost everything. You're not going to get picked on anymore. And don't forget: you've got nobody bossing you around all the time. Plus you have a nice family, a good home, and plenty of food to eat."

"I'm not sure you can call this *food*," I interrupted, shooting a sour glance at my lunchbox.

Jeannine just ignored me.

"Best of all, you have exciting adventures other kids can only dream about. And you have one really good friend. I'd say you have it pretty good."

I still scowled at her.

"No," I finally said, but then my scowl cracked and fell from my face. "No, I have it *great*."

And then big smiles broke across both of our faces.

"I guess what Bigelow always says is right," I pondered. "Everything depends on what you focus on."

"Personally," Jeannine said gleefully, "I'm focusing on that piece of strawberry cheesecake you have packed in your lunchbox."

I laughed.

"You do know that my *mother* made that," I pointed out as she pulled the slice out of the box and began unwrapping.

"And that she made it out of tofu and goat cheese."

Jeannine borrowed my fork and cut off a piece, then drew it to her nose. She hesitated a moment and sniffed it suspiciously, but then put it in her mouth and closed her eyes. I'm pretty sure I saw her grimace a little.

"Well?" I asked.

Jeannine smiled.

"Well, it's way better than the pickled Brussels Sprouts in *my* lunch box."

I laughed again.

"My mom's cooking, or a vegetable that looks and tastes like something grown in one of the dark circles of Hades," I chortled. "Some choice."

"Sometimes," Jeannine said as she finally opened her eyes, "those are the only kinds of choices we have."

I picked up the bag of what looked like green turds that was in Jeannine's lunchbox.

"Pickled Brussels Sprouts?" I grimaced.

"My mother calls it 'an acquired taste'," Jeannine explained. "That means…"

"It's horrible," I finished. "But you might learn to like it. My dad says the same thing about liverwurst."

"And is it true?" Jeannine asked.

I looked at her, and then back at the mottled green sprouts.

"I guess we'll see…eventually," I answered. And then I popped one of those vegetables from Hades, whole and unsparingly, into my mouth.

The adventure continues in

Will Allen and the Terrible Truth

He's conquered monsters –
He's overcome bullies –
He's even survived his mother's cooking –

But in his next trial, monster detective Will Allen must face a challenge that even with all of his bravery, cleverness, and skill, he is woefully inept at :

Dealing with girls!

For a full preview of this and all other **Chronicles of the Monster Detective Agency** volumes, as well as character profiles, games, and loads of other extras, visit our website, **MonsterDetectiveAgency.com**!

Award-winning Author/Educator Jason Edwards has over 25 year of experience developing innovative ways to entertain, instruct, and inspire young people. He travels all over the country performing his acclaimed, library skills-building **Monster Hunt** program and his **Destination: INSPIRATION** story crafting workshop at hundreds of schools, libraries, and book festivals. His talents have been featured across the nation on television, radio, print, and the internet.

Jason lives in New York with his wife and children. For more information about Jason and his programs, or to inquire about his availability, visit us on the web at RogueBearPress.com or contact Jason via e-mail at: Jason@RogueBearPress.com